SAVAGE HOLIDAY

Books by Richard Wright

Uncle Tom's Children

Native Son

Uncle Tom's Children: Five Long Stories

Native Son (The Biography of a Young American):
A Play in Ten Scenes. With Paul Green

Bright and Morning Star

12 Million Black Voices

Black Boy: A Record of Childhood and Youth

Cinque Uomini

The Outsider

Savage Holiday

Black Power: A Record of Reaction
in a Land of Pathos

The Color Curtain: A Report
on the Bandung Conference

Pagan Spain

White Man, Listen!

The Long Dream

Eight Men

Lawd Today

American Hunger

Richard Wright Reader

Early Works: Lawd Today,
Uncle Tom's Children, Native Son

Later Works: Black Boy (American Hunger),
The Outsider

SAVAGE
HOLIDAY

A Novel by
Richard Wright

With an afterword by
Gerald Early

Banner Books
University Press of Mississippi/Jackson

First published in 1954 by Avon
Copyright © 1954 by Richard Wright
Afterword copyright © 1994
by the University Press of Mississippi
Reprinted by arrangement
with John Hawkins & Associates, Inc., New York
All rights reserved
Manufactured in the United States of America

97   96   95   94   4   3   2   1

Library of Congress Cataloging-in-Publication Data

Wright, Richard, 1908-1960.
    Savage holiday : a novel / by Richard Wright ; with an
afterword by Gerald Early.
        p. cm. — (Banner books)
    ISBN 0-87805-749-8. — ISBN 0-87805-750-1 (pbk.)
    1. White men—New York (N.Y.)—Psychology—Fiction.
I. Title. II. Series: Banner books (Jackson, Miss.)
PS3545. R815S28   1995
813'.52 — dc20   94-35500
                                                      CIP

British Library Cataloging-in-Publication data available

Dedication
to

CLINTON BREWER

CONTENTS

For he who sins a second time,
Wakes a dead soul to pain,
And draws it from its spotted shroud,
And makes it bleed again,
And makes it bleed great gouts of blood,
And makes it bleed in vain!
                    —Oscar Wilde's **The Ballad of Reading Gaol**

And, behold, there came a great wind from the wilder-
ness, and smote the four corners of the house . . .
                    —Job, 1:19

PART 1: ANXIETY

Six days shalt thou labor, and do all thy
work: But the seventh day is the sabbath
of the Lord thy God: in it thou shalt not
do any work...
                                —Exodus, 20: 9, 10

Sunday is the holiday of present-day
civilized humanity... But it is not given
to everyone to vent their holiday wan-
tonness... freely and naturally.
    —Sandor Ferenczi's *Sunday Neuroses*

... in the very nature of a holiday there
is excess; the holiday mood is brought
about by the release of what is forbidden.
                        —Freud's *Totem and Taboo*

A CASCADE of shimmering yellow light showered down from crystal chandeliers and drenched the faces of more than five hundred men and women dining at the long, resplendent banquet tables in the Jefferson Banquet Salon of one of New York's largest and most luxurious mid-town hotels. Like a fabulously gaudy canopy, red, black, and gold streamers of twisted paper crisscrossed the ceiling, festooned the walls, evoking an atmosphere that was rich, dense, and colorful.

On a wall to the right, spanning the length of the room, high up near the ceiling, was strung a huge, white, eye-catching banner whose modernistically blocked characters of red and blue proclaimed:

THE LONGEVITY LIFE INSURANCE COMPANY, INC.
GIRDS THE WORLD AND BRINGS
Security to You and Your Survivors
Tonight We Tender a Fond
HAIL AND FAREWELL
to
ERSKINE FOWLER

FOR THIRTY YEARS OF EXEMPLARY SERVICE
AND DEVOTION

11

Near the center windows in the left wall and at a table decorated with a giant, spraying bouquet of long-stemmed roses sat a quiet, reserved group of men whose fleshy faces, massive bodies, gray and bald heads marked them as wealthy executives. One of them, a white-haired man whose forceful, ruddy face, China blue eyes, and squared chin gave him the demeanor of a tamed pirate, was speaking:

"And now, this doughty warrior, after thirty long years of care and toil, lays down his burden of responsibility and can honestly look any man in the eye and say, 'I've earned this rest of mine with the sweat of my brow—this is the end of a perfect day!'"

The speaker's hearers were visibly moved and the handclapping was as soft, as shy, as the rustling of tree leaves in a spring wind.

"Brothers and sisters, just think—Erskine Fowler looked upon Longevity Life as his family! Ah, I remember him years ago—though it seems to my mind's eye that it was but yesterday!—running errands, learning the ropes, figuring the angles, growing up with a growing company, becoming a Mason, a Rotarian, a Sunday School Superintendent, a man of parts ... What a miracle life is! What a tremendous boon we have been to this man, and what a godsend he has been to us! What a collaboration! What a partnership! What a fulfillment of promise ... !"

Applause, strident, deafening ...

"Brothers and sisters, thirty years is a long, long span of time:—Time enough to cap the hair of a head like mine with silver frost. ... Time enough for countless souls to be chastened in the valley of suffering. ... Time enough for Almighty God to lay His final Hand upon some of us. ... Time enough for millions of new faces to make their God-given appearance here on earth in our midst. ... Time enough for war

... Time enough for peace ... Time enough for sorrow ... Time enough for a little happiness ... But,
never forget, time enough for devotion, for service,
for character building, for brotherly love ..."

The speaker's voice quavered under the stress of
emotion. A few scattered handclaps began, timid
and hesitant; then, gathering courage, the crowd
lifted their applause to a crescendo that went on and
on until the white-haired man finally stemmed the
flood with his uplifted palms.

"Brothers and sisters of the Longevity Family, I'm
not here to make a speech tonight. I want simply as
president, or head of this family, to make manifest to
the world that if Erskine Fowler has served us well,
we want him and the world to know it.

"Last month our Board of Directors voted unanimously to have a special medal of gold struck in his
honor.

"Long and earnestly we debated in choosing the
words to be inscribed upon that medal." Amid silence,
the speaker paused, took from an inside coat pocket
a flat, black box and, opening it, gazed for a moment
at something which his audience could not see. "One
side of this medal of gold bears the profile of Erskine
Fowler, and the opposite side—" He paused again,
turned the medal in the flat box, and continued:
"... bears these simple, heartfelt words which I'll
read if Erskine Fowler will be so kind as to stand
up ..."

A six-foot, hulking, heavy, muscular man with a
Lincoln-like, quiet, stolid face, deep-set brown eyes,
a jutting lower lip, a shock of jet-black, bushy hair,
rose nervously, ran his left hand tensely inside of his
coat (as though touching something), brushed his
right hand across his chin, then let his fingers, which
trembled slightly, rest upon the table in front of him.

His facial features seemed hewn firm and whole from some endurable substance; his eyes were steady; he was the kind of man to whom one intuitively and readily rendered a certain degree of instant deference, not because there was anything challenging, threatening, or even strikingly intelligent in those carelessly molded and somewhat blunted features; but because one immediately felt that he was superbly alive, real, just *there*, with no hint in his attitude of apology for himself or his existence, confident of his inalienable right to confront you and demand his modest due of respect.... He looked confoundingly younger than his forty-three years; indeed, one would easily have taken him to be thirty-five or -six. ... He stood with a fixed, embarrassed smile and his brown eyes shone with the moisture of emotion.

The speaker cleared his throat and declaimed: "Erskine Fowler, the Board of Directors, the President, and the officials, and more than five thousand employees of the Longevity Life Insurance Company declare unto you: 'WELL DONE, THOU FAITHFUL STEWARD OF OUR TRUST!'"

Spontaneously, as one man, the crowd gained its feet and gave vent to prolonged cheering. The speaker extended to Erskine Fowler's left hand the flat, black box containing the gold medal; next he seized Erskine Fowler's right hand and shook it with vigor, then clapped him in a fatherly way on the back, pronouncing: "God bless and keep you, Erskine!"

"Thank you, Mr. Warren," the recipient said, in a half-whisper.

"Show it! Let's see it!" Sundry voices rang out.

There were yells, whistles, stomping of feet. A maudlin mood seized the crowd. Erskine Fowler, with pride, timidity, and even an element of fear gleaming in his face, tiptoed and lifted the flat box high above his head and turned it to left and right, allowing the soft sheen of the golden disc to shed its lustrous benediction upon all eyes. His movements were stiff and constrained, as though he were acting against his will.

"Higher, higher ... !"

Erskine Fowler forced a smile. A lusty singing broke out and, a moment later, the orchestra underscored the full-bodied strains:

> *For he's a jolly good fellow*
> *For he's a jolly good fellow*
> *For he's a jolly good fellow*
> *Which nobody can deny ...*

Erskine Fowler's fingers shook; he fumbled clumsily with the flat black box and laid it on the table before him. His lips quivered; then he could no longer check the turbulence of his emotions. As the clapping rose louder and higher, profuse tears seeped from his eyes and etched their way slowly down his cheeks. Erskine Fowler drew forth his handkerchief, balled it, and dabbed fumblingly, trying to dry his eyes. Some of the young, dewey-eyed stenographers crooned:

"Aw look ... ! That's so cute! He's *crying* ... !"

There were masculine shouts:

"Speech! Speech!"

Erskine Fowler brought himself under control; he hunched his huge shoulders a bit forward, made a slight, nervous, upward-shrugging motion with his arms and elbows close to his body, as though hitching up his trousers before going into combat, and set his face resolutely toward the crowd. He lifted his hands for silence and a soft chorus of "Sssshss" went around the room. When all was quiet, Erskine Fowler turned with slow and serious dignity toward Mr. Warren, bowed, and, in a rich, charged baritone, began:

"Mr. President, members of the Board of Directors, brothers and sisters of the Longevity Family:—What can I say? Truly, my heart's full to overflowing. As all of you know, I'm no speechmaker. My command of words is meager. Action is my forte, and I'm at a loss when called upon to express myself. . . . But, believe me, I'm not unmindful of, or insensible to, the great tribute that is being tendered to me tonight. Yet, if I may, with your permission, I'd like, so to speak, to turn the tables and pay a tribute to Mr. Warren, the Board of Directors, and to my thousands of co-workers who have made my services with the Longevity Life so pleasant and inspiring. It's to you that I feel I owe thanks . . ."

Quiet handclapping . . .

"You know, as well as I, that in a strictly physical sense we have come to the parting of ways, but in a wider, deeper sense we can never really part. We will continue to commune together through what that great savior of our country, Abraham Lincoln, called the 'better angels of our nature'!

"Brothers and sisters, it's a poignant feeling that haunts me tonight. Leave-taking is always such a melancholy business. Really, words fail me at this moment . . ." Erskine Fowler swallowed, blinked; the strain of emotion pulled at the muscles in his face. With a reflex gesture, he inserted his left hand to his inner coat pocket, as though to make sure that he had not lost something, then he continued: "Yet I possess no small degree of pride for, no matter how humble my capacities really were, I did lend a willing hand in building up this our common monument of business. But what we achieved was not merely all business. As our great President has so often pointed out, and I heartily agree with him, millions of people depend upon us for their welfare, come to us in their bereavement, and seek us out in their hope ... That's not business; that's *faith!*"

A ripple of handclapping ... A sharp, tense struggle seemed to reflect itself in Erskine Fowler's face; he mastered himself quickly, suddenly laughed, tossed his head roguishly, shot a shy, darting glance at Mr. Warren, and then recommenced in a lilting, jocular manner:

"I'm retiring at what is a rather unusually early age, but don't kid yourself! Sure; I'm forty-three; but, by golly, I feel that I'm twenty-three! There's a hell of a lot of kick left in this old mule yet!"

Laughter, shouts, even some whistling ...

"Tell 'em, Erskine!"

"Yeah!"

"Don't give up, boy!"

"Sure; I'm retiring, but not out of action! I'm smiling and moving into the reserve ranks ... !"

"Atta boy!"

"We're with you, Erskine!"

"Now, don't you think that because I'm retiring, that I'm going to stop living," Erskine Fowler warned them, shaking a threatening forefinger. "Why, I haven't even begun living yet!" He banged the table with his fist.

More handclapping ...

"I'm deeply loath to sever my ties with this splendid organization." He switched to a sober note, speaking in a husky whisper. "But, when one has served his time, he must go. Yet the sun's not setting for me ... I beg leave, with all due respect, to correct a statement of our beloved President. He spoke of this being, for me, the end of a perfect day! No; no . . . No; my friends! It's high noon! Not only for me, but for Longevity Life!"

Erskine Fowler saw Mr. Warren lean forward, break into a smile, and nod his approval as more handclapping beat through the air. Erskine Fowler's face flushed and became darkly pugnacious as he argued:

"The Board of Directors has voted to retain me in the capacity of a consulting advisor." He turned and faced Mr. Warren. "Mr. President, sir, let me caution you that I'm going to be a mighty disappointed man if my phone doesn't ring one of these mornings soon and I don't hear you telling me: 'Erskine, I want you to get right down here at once; there's something terribly important I want you to do!'"

Amid something akin to pandemonium, Mr. Warren rose hastily and rushed to Erskine Fowler's side, took hold of his shoulder and spun him round with affectionate rudeness. With cheers deafening their ears, the two men confronted each other, immobile, silent; then Mr. Warren flung wide his arms in a gesture of receiving to his heart a brother whom he would never deny. Elaborately he embraced Erskine Fowler and patted him tenderly on the back with both of his palms. When the cheering had subsided, Mr. Warren informed Erskine Fowler in tones that carried throughout the room:

"You bet your sweet life I'll call you, Erskine; and by God, when I do, you'd *better* come!"

Staring solemnly into each other's eyes, they shook hands. Erskine Fowler was moving his lips, trying to say something, but he could not get his words past the constriction in his throat. In the end he simply nodded his head and his eyes were dripping wet . . .

A tall, gray-haired man sprang to his feet, his right

hand raised, and called out above the tumult: "Mr. President! Mr. President!"

The noise abated a bit.

"Yes, Mr. Edwards," Mr. Warren answered.

"Mr. President," the gray-haired man began as the room quieted, "I hope that I'm not out of order. And, assuming that I'm not, I hereby move that an account of these honorable proceedings be published in the next issue, along with suitable photographs, of our official journal, *Longevity Life . . . !*"

A stout, red-faced man rose and boomed: "I second that motion!"

With his arm still draped about Erskine Fowler's shoulders, Mr. Warren proclaimed: "It has been moved and seconded that a full account of the honorable proceedings of this august ceremony be commemorated with proper dignity in the pages of our official journal, *Longevity Life*. Is there any discussion on this motion?"

"Question! Question!" rose from several throats.

"If there's no discussion, I ask all who are in favor of this motion to signify their assent by saying, 'Yes'!"

"YYYEEESSSSS!" a growl of approval thundered from the crowd.

"Those opposed!" Mr. Warren called.

Silence.

"The motion is carried unanimously!" Mr. Warren shouted, both of his palms stretching upwards with fingers spread.

A young woman dressed in a white suit came briskly forward with camera and flashbulb and, stooping and sighting, sent three flashes of blue lightning into Erskine Fowler's and Mr. Warren's face.

Erskine Fowler stood uncertainly, blinking; then, overcome, he sat abruptly. A storm of whistling, stomping, and yelling rang in his ears and there was an abortive attempt to sing *For He's a Jolly Good Fellow* again; but the orchestra, at a signal from one of the executives, filled the room with a popular waltz tune and the waiters hurriedly began removing the tables and chairs. Erskine Fowler watched dazedly as dancing couples, smiling and looking at him, began to swing undulatingly past his eyes that swam in tears . . .

He felt lost, abandoned; he was alone amidst it all. Time was flowing pitilessly on; Longevity Life would keep marching, and he was on the outside of it all, standing on the sidelines, rejected, refused; he swallowed and dried his eyes again. Suddenly he felt that he could endure no more of it; he rose and mumbled hoarsely:

"Excuse me, please. I'll be back in a moment . . ."

He headed toward the men's room, his eyes on the floor, walking slowly. Several men clapped him heartily on the back and called out their congratulations. Erskine Fowler forced himself to smile at them . . .

Yes; Erskine had fled. He had taken himself out of their sight, had broken his promise to remain until the end of the banquet. A sudden sense of outrage had made him decide that he would no longer be a party to his own defeat. . . . As he made his way down the corridor toward the stairway, anger burned in him so hot and hard that his vision blurred. When he had declared to that array of upturned faces that "leave-taking is always such a melancholy business," he had not been speaking at random or rhetorically. Indeed, he had had to rein himself in, while facing that crowd, to keep from bursting out with the true facts, to keep from screaming to the public that the whole thing was a farce, a put-up job! And what was now making him so angry and disgusted with himself was that, at the last moment, instead of hurling a monkey wrench into Warren's smoothly organized machinery of falsehood, he had had a failure of nerve, had collaborated in the game of make-believe.

The urge to expose to his co-workers the hidden reasons for his leaving Longevity Life had clashed with his pledged word to hold his tongue, and the resulting tension had so tautened his muscles that he could not have endured any more of that ceremony without actually collapsing temporarily. His sitting there at his table so quietly and knowing that within an hour a thirty-years' relationship would, against his will and in spite of his protest, irrevocably terminate had been like watching a knife whose sharp edge of blade was nearing a bared nerve. . . .

To avoid meeting his erstwhile associates, he sought to leave the hotel by a side entrance. He came to the head of a rear stairway and paused, gazing broodingly down at the descending sweep of wide, carpeted steps. He was alone. Slowly his left hand reached inside his coat and his fingers touched the tip ends of a row of four automatic pencils— black, red, blue, and green—clipped to an inner pocket. Whenever he was distraught or filled with anxiety, he invariably made this very same compulsive gesture which he had developed in some obscure and forgotten crisis in his past; his touching those pencils always somehow reassured him, for they seemed to symbolize an inexplicable need to keep contact with some emotional resolution whose meaning and content he did not know. . . .

Yes; his leaving that banquet had been indefensible and irrational. He had not only broken his promise to Warren to stick it out, but he had revealed himself as a man who could not keep a grip upon himself. Yet he knew that his running out had another and deeper meaning. In fleeing from that banquet room, he had been really trying to flee from himself; that banquet room had been but an objective symbolization of a reality which he, at that moment, had wanted more than anything else on this earth to avoid. And the reality that had so frightened him was so completely himself and his own past life that he could only feel it, suffer it; he couldn't know it, master it . . .

Squeezing the flat box in his right palm, he crept down the stairs like a criminal. He'd been discarded, scrapped; he was outdated, no longer of any use to the company he'd helped to build. Sure; he could easily get another job; he was known far and wide in the insurance world as an A-1 executive, as a cracker-jack who always delivered the goods. But that wasn't the point. He knew Longevity Life from A to Z, better than he knew himself, and to see his own company toss away a man of his value—he was sure that he'd have felt the same way about it if it had been someone else!—made him furious. He wanted to spit as he recalled those lying, oily phrases spewing from Warren's thin lips—Warren, who had wanted him out of the way *more* than any of the others! He was deadwood that they'd gotten rid of; he'd been pensioned off. True; he'd drawn a handsome batch of dollars as severance pay; but they'd wanted him out of the way just the same.

But, by God, he'd show 'em! They thought that he was old-fashioned, a washout. He'd find another position; no; not right away; he'd look around first; and when he did find another job, he'd make such a name for himself, he'd be such a whizz that Longevity Life would wish that they'd never let him go. . . . They made me take a bribe, he told himself bitterly. But they'll regret it. He wouldn't be at all surprised if, after a year, they called him back . . .

Even though that bylaw, which had enabled the Board of Directors, at its own discretion, to compel the retirement of any employee who had thirty years or more of service, had been enacted more than two years ago, his obsessive conviction of having been unfairly dealt with, unfeelingly lopped off, made him now suspect that they had had him especially in mind when they had voted it.

But what had stung his ego most of all was that Miss Cramer, his loyal ex-secretary, had told him this morning at the office—making him swear on his honor that he'd never breathe a word of it to a living soul—that Robert Warren, President Albert Warren's youngest son—just turned twenty-three years of age!— (Young enough to be my son! Erskine had exclaimed to himself!) was taking over his work as the district manager for Manhattan.... So it was not only because they thought him inefficient, not because he wasn't liked and respected by everybody, that he was being dumped; it was to make a place for his son that Warren was giving him the air! Robert Warren was going to be married and old man Warren was making Robert the district manager of Manhattan as a wedding present!

Erskine remembered having seen the kid, Robert, a few times, sometimes on the street and sometimes around the office; and had not seen, on those occasions, anything distinctive or exceptional about him. Just a good-looking, jolly youngster flashing up and down the avenues in his sport model, convertible Buick with a tall, blonde girl ... Once or twice he'd read in the gossip columns about young Warren's being at this or that nightclub. But *never* would Erskine have thought that such a harmless, money-spending brat would have been selected to replace him ... And that hare-brained girl he was marrying

...A fumigated tart, no doubt...The injustice of it made him want to vomit.

All afternoon before the banquet he had sat in his apartment by his telephone, fuming, trying to summon up enough courage to phone Warren and have it out with him. But, despite his raw anger, he hadn't been able to act. He had thought of sending Warren a wire and calling off the banquet, but he hadn't been inventive enough to think of iron-clad reasons for such an action—reasons that could be made public...Night had found him still seething and undecided.

But when he'd reached the hotel, knowing that within an hour his last chance to protest would be gone, he'd taken the bit into his teeth and had demanded a short conference with Warren and the crusty, acid-tongued vice president, Ricky. The showdown had taken place in a tiny room off the banquet hall behind closed doors, and no sooner had Erskine looked into their grim and determined faces than he had become swamped with doubts and had regretted his rashness.

"Well, Erskine, what's on your mind?" Warren had broken the ice, speaking through a lying smile.

Erskine had swallowed and wished to God that he'd not asked for such an audience. But what had he to lose? By the living God, he'd let them know what he thought of such cowardly deception! He *had* to protest their abandonment of him...

"Why didn't you tell me that you wanted me out to make a place for your son?" he had demanded of Warren with more bluntness than he had intended.

Warren had paled, his lips parted, and he looked at Ricky and turned away, shaking his head. It had been Ricky who had taken up the fight.

"Fowler, aren't you stepping just a bit outside of

your little track?" Ricky had asked with cool in-
solence.

"Look, don't play games with me," Erskine had
said. "I know what the score is. And this is a cheap,
sickening way to treat a man who's given his life to
this company..."

"We're not interested in your opinions, Fowler,"
Warren had said.

"I think you *are* interested," Erskine had put in.
"Or else you'd have been man enough to have told
me what was up. No; you wanted to ease me out—"

"Fowler, are you mad, man?" Ricky had bawled
at him. "We've *settled* this! You promised you'd go!
The hell with the reasons... Now, why do you bring
up this matter half an hour before the banquet...?"

"Because I found out the trick you're playing on
me," Erskine argued. "You didn't dare tell me—"

"So what?" Warren had demanded. "Fowler, you're
off balance, boy! Don't overestimate yourself!"

"Look here, Fowler." Ricky had let his voice drop
to a neutral, almost kindly tone. "You've got severance pay. You own some stock in the company. To
all intents, so far as the public is concerned, you're
being retired with your consent. You're being kept
on as an advisor. You're drawing a pension... We're
giving you a public banquet. What in hell more do
you want?"

"Honesty!" Erskine had shouted. "I just want you
to be straight with me, just as I've been with you!"

"Fowler, the banquet room's filling up... People
are waiting... You can't back out now... Be honorable—" Warren had argued gently.

"Where's *your* honor?" Erskine had asked in a
frenzy.

"Look, I'll help you get another position," Warren

had said. "Be reasonable, man. Nobody's disputing your loyalty—"

"Who told you about Robert Warren's taking your place?" Ricky had asked pointedly.

"Never mind," Erskine had said. "So, this is how you felt all along, hunh?"

"All right," Ricky had snarled. "You're asking for it, by God, and I'm going to give it to you. You're *through*, Fowler; hear? You're out of date, behind the times; get it? We want live wires with gray matter upstairs; see? Maybe we ought to have put you wise long ago.... All right; you're good, Fowler. But, goddammit, you're not good *enough!* You just don't have what we want! Do you want me to spell it out any clearer? Now, go out there and do what you promised! If you back out now—"

"WE'LL FIRE YOU!" Warren had shouted in a brutal rage. "We'll *kick* you out! Embarrass us tonight, after we treat you like a right guy, and we'll..." Warren's face had turned a deep red. "Don't you cross me, Fowler. We've been damned good to you. Now, *you* play straight."

Humiliation had choked Erskine and he'd known that he'd been licked. He'd burned his bridges; the gulf that had yawned so nakedly between them would never have been so glaring had he kept his mouth shut. Ricky's thin lips had been shut tight, like a trap; and Warren's China-blue eyes had gleamed as cold and blue as twin icebergs. And at that moment the nervous, discordant sounds of the musicians' instruments being tuned up in the banquet room had come to him. Erskine's legs had trembled. Ricky had reached out suddenly and had clutched hold of Erskine's arm and had pushed him roughly against a wall.

"If you don't go through with this, you're out

without even a recommendation," Ricky had said. "Do you want to fight Longevity Life?"

"No," Erskine had breathed, wilting.

"That's just what you're doing, and I warn you!" Warren had told him.

"But ... but ..." Erskine's voice had stuck in his throat.

He'd longed to send his right fist smashing into Warren's face; instead, as though performing a ceremonial gesture of penance, his left hand had nervously reached inside his coat and felt the tips of the four pencils clipped there ... For almost five minutes the three of them had stood wordlessly in the tiny, closed room, fronting one another but avoiding one another's eyes, and in the background there was that faint, discordant plunking of a violin, the insistent sounding of the keys of A, B flat, and C on the piano ...

"Well, dammit, what're you going to do?" Ricky had demanded.

Impulsively, Erskine had moved toward the door; he'd not known just where he was going; he'd just wanted to get out of their presence. Tall, strong Ricky had grabbed his shoulder and had spun him round.

"Don't strike me, Ricky," Erskine had muttered, his eyes narrowing.

"You're not walking out of here without giving us an answer," Ricky had said, taking his hand from Erskine's shoulder.

Erskine had hung his head. For twenty years he had worshipped these men, and now they were hating him.

"Okay; I'm through," he had mumbled, swallowing.

"If you want to put it that way," Warren had said. "You're going to play your part?"

"Okay. I'll play my part," Erskine had said with a sigh; he had not looked up.

There wasn't anything more to be said. The harmonious strain of a waltz wafted to them.

"All right; let's get going," Ricky had said.

Erskine had marched slowly out of the room between Warren and Ricky; he'd felt that he was an animal being flanked by its two trainers. They were leading him toward the circus ring and, though he would snarl, bare his fangs, he was going to go through his paces. . . .

Erskine reached the bottom of the stairs and let his eyes rove over the crowded rear lobby. Yes; that scene of degradation would live in his heart to his dying hour. They hadn't even been sympathetic enough to say: "We know how you feel, Erskine . . ." They were streamlining and modernizing the organization and they had replaced him with young Warren who was from Harvard and had studied insurance scientifically . . .

"They've gone hogwild and haywire over new ideas and methods," he mumbled to himself. "And they don't know what insurance really is . . ."

Erskine was unalterably convinced that there was nothing that any university could instill in anybody that could remotely match his own superb, practical knowledge of insurance. Insurance was life itself; insurance was human nature in the raw trying to hide itself; insurance was instinctively and intuitively knowing that man was essentially a venal, deluded, and greedy animal . . .

Yes; insurance was a shifty-eyed, timid, sensual, sluttish woman trying, with all of her revolting and nauseating sexiness, to make you believe that she'd been maimed for life in an automobile accident, and you wouldn't, couldn't believe her or take her word for it, or take her doctor's word for it, and you'd smiled at her and led her to believe that you believed her and you easily beat her at her crooked game by just looking into her eyes and letting her fool herself into thinking that maybe you were falling for her, and, in the end, you'd trapped her into admitting that she was lying and you settled her claim for one-tenth of what her itchy palms had been wanting . . .

Yes; insurance was a small-time, stupid, greasy-faced Italian grocery-store keeper who had amateurishly set his dingy, garlic-reeking place ablaze hoping that he'd collect enough insurance money to start all over again under another name and in another state, and you'd talked to the dope for fifteen minutes and had caught him in such a tangle of contradictions that he'd gotten frightened and had confessed and was eventually sent to prison for five years . . .

Yes; insurance was an old, sweet-looking woman of seventy-odd who'd insured her new daughter-in-law for a huge amount of money and then had, with a stout hatchet, killed her one night in her bed and had told a seemingly plausible tale of having awakened from her sleep and having seen a tall, dark man (Erskine was convinced that all "tall, dark men" were but the figments of guilty women's imagination!) fleeing down the dark hallway of their frame house and of immediately afterwards hearing groans in her daughter-in-law's bedroom and of finding her daughter-in-law in bed hacked to pieces and soaking in blood, and you had from the first doubted the sweet-looking old woman's sobbing story and a few days later, while rummaging about the house with an inspector from the company, had found the old woman's bloody nightgown wrapped around a brand-new hatchet and balled stiffly and stuffed into a corner of her clothes closet, and you had confronted the old woman and had argued gently with her for hours and had made her sob out her crime and had, moreover, made her see and know that she had sinned . . .

Yes; insurance was something you just couldn't learn out of books, not matter how thick and profound they were. You just had to *know* in your heart that man was a guilty creature . . .

"But, how *do* you know, Erskine?" his astonished colleagues used to ask him.

Erskine would wag his head, smile, and mumble: "There's just something in me that listens to a person when he talks and *it* tells me when he's guilty."

"You've got a lot of horse sense," they'd said.

But he knew that it was something infinitely more mysterious than horse sense that made him so knowing. In fact, his uncanny shrewdness was an odd side of him, bringing blessings as well as bane, shoring him with confidence as well as sapping his sleep at night, exerting its influence over a far wider area of his life than just the insurance business. His knowing intuitions not only made him uncommonly profound in detecting the pretenses of others, but sometimes it created odd situations in which he became incredibly obtuse, stupid almost.

His unsteady legs carried him across the lobby to the hotel door. So, it was over—this night which he had dreaded for so long. He sighed and stepped to the sidewalk; a wall of humid heat hit his face and his breathing became shallow as he stood uncertainly amid the passers-by. That infernal air-conditioning was now making him dizzy as he tried to adjust himself to the sudden rise in temperature. Why didn't people leave natural things alone? Why were they forever tinkering and changing things? Yeah; they'd always regarded him as a little queer in the office because he wouldn't exclaim and wax slobberingly enthusiastic over every new gadget. Well, at least I'm free of their taunting me behind my back.... And they'd miss him; of that, he was sure. Why, things'd get so snarled up in the office that in a week they'd phone him and beg him to come back and straighten them out. Ah, and just wait until the next quarterly dividends were declared! He'd bet a cool, even hundred bucks that they'd be somewhat lower. They couldn't help but be lower with his not being there to spot the phonies and cut corners ... Bad business! Erskine pronounced his judgment as he plodded through the Saturday-night crowd.

He knew, however, that his bitter tirades against his former colleagues were but a crude camouflage covering his real dilemma. What was fundamentally fretting him was that—now that he'd retired and was free—he didn't know what to do with himself. His hated freedom was simply suspending him in a void of anxious ignorance that was riveting his consciousness with self-protective nostalgia upon the familiar atmosphere of the Longevity Life Insurance Company.

What, for example, did he want to do at this moment? Go to a movie? No. A movie would only distract him and he didn't want to be distracted. Read a book? No; no; God, no! He would have resented some novelist's trying to project him upon some foolish flight of fantasy. He could, of course, visit his favorite bowling alley; but he was not inclined to sweat out the poisons of his tired body tonight ... The alien thorns that were nestling in him went far

deeper than the flesh...Then, what was he to
do...?

A subtle sense of terror, potent but vague, seeped
into his soul and the night's damp heat made sweat
beads on his upper lip. Yes, God; *this* was that un-
welcome, uncanny, haunting sensation against which
he had to employ all his emotional energies now;
the dodging, the eluding of *this* nameless and invisible enemy had gripped and preoccupied him more
and more since his life had turned from a settled
routine into a nagging problem. He was plagued
by a jittery premonition that some monstrous and
hoary recollection, teasing him and putting his teeth
on edge because it was strange and yet somehow
familiar, was about to break disastrously into his
consciousness. He blinked his eyes, shook his head,
touched the tips of his four pencils in his inner coat
pocket to free himself of these filmy cobwebs dust-
ing at his mind...A red traffic light made him halt
and he felt the hot pavement vibrating beneath his
feet as a subway train sped through the underground.
Nervously he slipped the flat, black box holding his
gold medal into his outer coat pocket and swabbed
his face with his handkerchief. He sighed, angry
and repelled by this haunting sense of not quite
being his own master.

Work had not only given Erskine his livelihood
and conferred upon him the approval of his fellow-
men; but, above all, it made him a stranger to a
part of himself that he feared and wanted never to
know. At some point in his childhood he had assumed toward himself the role of a policeman, had
accused himself, had hauled himself brutally into the
court of his conscience, had arraigned himself before
the bar of his fears, and had found himself guilty and
had, finally and willingly, dragged himself off to

serve a sentence of self-imposed labor for life, had locked himself up in a prison-cage of toil ... Now, involuntarily reprieved, each week six full new Sundays suddenly loomed terrifyingly before him and he had to find a way to outwit that rejected part of him that Longevity Life had helped to incarcerate so long and successfully. He was trapped in freedom. How could he again make a foolproof prison of himself for all of his remaining days? What invisible walls could he now erect about his threatening feelings, desires? How could he suppress or throttle those slow and turgid stirrings of buried impulses now trying to come to resurrected life in the deep dark of him? How could he become his own absolute jailer and keep the peace within the warring precincts of his heart?

The majority of men, timid and unthinking, obey the laws and mandates of society because they yearn to merit the esteem and respect of their law-abiding neighbors. Still others, reflective and conscious, obey because they are intelligently afraid of the reprisals meted out by society upon the breakers of the law. There are still other men of a deeper and more sensitive nature who, in their growing up, introject the laws and mandates of society into their hearts and come in time to feel and accept these acquired notions of right and wrong as native impulses springing out of the depths of their beings and, if they are ever tempted to violate these absorbed codes, act as though the sky itself were about to crash upon their heads, as though the very earth were about to swing catastrophically out of its orbit ...

Such a man was Erskine Fowler, but the laws and mandates which he had introjected into his heart were of a special sort, and were unknown to him until, one day, time accidentally exposed what they were ...

But, now, to avoid the commission of what crime—or had the crime already been committed and was he trying to escape its memory?—was Erskine hankering so anxiously to imprison himself? What had he ever done—or what did he fear doing?—that made him feel so positively that he had to encircle himself, his heart, and his actions with bars, to hold himself in leash?

The air was close and humid. It was nearing midnight; the traffic and the passers-by had lessened. He walked, brooding.

Reaching home, he rode up in the automatic elevator to the tenth floor of the Elmira apartment building which was located in the upper Seventies of Manhattan; he entered a bedroom that had never been dishonored by the presence of a stray woman of pleasure. Undressing, he assured himself that he'd soon solve the problem of his enforced leisure; that his general state of mind was all right; that he was a good man, honest, kind, clean, straight—the kind of man who loved children. Why, take that little five-year-old Tony Blake who lived next door ... He'd given that child so much ice cream and so many toys that his mother, Mrs. Blake, a shapely, plump, brunette war-widow, was astonished and blushed when trying to stammer her gratitude.

On occasion Mrs. Blake herself, with her easy, flashing smile, had caught his timid fancy. She was comely, as alone as he was and, at odd moments, he'd found himself wondering about her. Once, on a summer Sunday morning—he'd been brewing coffee in the kitchen—he'd caught a glimpse of her clad only in panties and brassiere and the image had lingered in his consciousness for days, confounding him with its drastic persistency. Another time, one summer evening, just before getting into bed, he'd seen her completely nude through the open window of his bedroom. That time he'd nipped in the bud the possibility of any such image haunting his mind by promptly becoming angry. "She doesn't have to be so blasted careless, does she?" For a week after that he'd not treated little Tony to any dishes of ice cream at the corner drugstore. It was not until Tony's puzzled, accusing eyes had reproached him that he'd resumed his role of the big father scattering gifts.

He showered, climbed into bed, and sighed; he had to rise early in the morning and do his duty at Sunday School. But he couldn't sleep; he tossed restlessly on the hot mattress, wondering what he would do with himself on Monday. Minnie, his colored maid, would be in the apartment and he'd hate her to see him at loose ends, pacing to and fro.

Through his open window he heard Mrs. Blake's phone ring once, twice, three times ... She's not in, he thought. She sure received a lot of telephone calls. He'd heard vaguely (was it from Mrs. Westerman, the wife of the building superintendent?) that she worked nights; but what kind of work ... ? And little Tony remained alone all night. What a mother! No wonder so many people in this world got into trouble; they didn't get the proper kind of guidance in their childhood. Women who couldn't give the right kind of attention to children oughtn't to be allowed to have them. Well, Mrs. Blake was a war-widow; that excused her some. But, nevertheless, a child of five oughtn't to be left alone all night ...

The night air was warm, heavy, motionless; he sighed and tossed on the hot sheet. Mrs. Blake's

phone rang six times. Some man, no doubt . . . Suppose the building caught fire? Why, poor Tony
would be trapped . . .

His eyelids drooped and soon he was breathing
regularly. A shifting curtain of wobbly images hovered before his consciousness; the images slowly
grew in density and solidity; he was in another
world, but he couldn't decide if he ought to accept
the images he saw in that world as real or not. He
turned, flung off the top sheet, swallowed, and
breathed rhythmically again. Yes; the images were
real and he allowed them to engage his emotions . . .

. . . He was walking down a narrow path bordered
by tall black weeds and then suddenly the path
widened into a strange, deep, dark forest with stal-
wart trees ranging on all sides of him and then he
was aware of treading upon dried leaves and twigs
and it came to him that he was tramping through
a vast, wooded area which he had just bought and
these majestic trees looming skyward were his own
and he was filled with a sense of pride as he tried
to see their vaulting branches whose heights soared
beyond his vision and then he paused and began
intricate mental calculations as to how much profit
he would make if he ordered all the trees cut down
and sawn into timber and shipped for sale to the
nearby city and he started counting the trees four
eight sixteen trees were in a space sixteen yards by
thirty-two yards and now he assumed that he had a
hundred acres of trees like these how much profit
would he realize but all of the trees were not of the
same size there were thicker and taller trees and he
pushed farther on into the forest and then he was
suddenly afraid and hid himself behind a large tree
and listened to the sound of *whack whack whack*
somebody was in the forest chopping down one of his

trees and he peered cautiously and saw a tall man swinging a huge ax chopping furiously into a v-shaped hollow of a giant tree and the chips were flying and the man's face was hard and brutish and criminal-looking and he was now resolved upon surprising the man and demanding that he get out of the forest and stop stealing his trees and he crept closer and saw that the man was about to cut straight through the tree and all at once the man stopped and whirled and saw him and yelled *run go quickly the tree's about to fall* and he looked up and saw the tall tree bending slowly and falling towards him and he heard the man yelling for him to run but he couldn't move his feet and when he looked up this time the tree was crashing down upon him and he managed to move at last trying to keep his eyes on the falling tree and he tripped on something and fell headlong and when he looked back to see where the falling tree was it was too late for the tree was upon him and he could feel the leaves and branches swishing and stinging his face and eyes and ears and then the crushing weight of the tree trunk smashed against his head ...

Bang bang bang came into Erskine's ears. He opened puffy eyes and blinked at the bright sunlight. Morning already? He was still sleepy. He turned his head and saw the towering tops of Manhattan's skyscrapers drenched in golden sunlight, but he was still staring at the strange dream images which were now fleeing from his consciousness. Again he heard that loud banging and he knew that Tony was beating his drum.

"That child," he muttered.

His watch told him that it was seven-thirty; Sunday School did not commence until nearly ten; he had time to doze again. He rolled over, closed his eyes ... Tony's yell came strident and piercing:

"Awhoo! Awhoo! Awhoo! The Indians are coming!"

She's sleeping and she lets that child bang and yell at this hour of the morning ... The child's noise ceased and he tucked his head deeper into his pillow and drifted into a semi-dream state, thinking of Tony who, in turn, made him recall dimly his own, faraway childhood. Yes; he too had once romped and played alone, yelling war whoops, and there'd been no mother to look after him either. Wasn't that maybe why he was so fond of Tony? And, too, wasn't it maybe because Mrs. Blake—alone, sensual, impulsive —was so much as he remembered his own mother that he found himself scolding her and brooding over her in his mind?

He had no memory of his father who had died when he was three years old; it was his mother whom he remembered or, rather, the images of the many men who always surrounded her laughing face—men who came and went, some indulgent toward him, some indifferent. Gradually, as he'd come to understand what was happening, he'd grown afraid, ashamed. They'd lived down in Atlanta then and the boys in the vacant lots and on the school grounds had flung cold, scornful words at him, and he'd been furious with his mother. Even now he winced with a dull, inner pain as he recalled his dreadful dilemma in trying to decide who deserved more to be killed for having behaved so that the boys on the playground could taunt him: ought the men be killed, or ought his mother be killed ... ?

Erskine shook his head, trying to stave off emotional scenes stemming from his childhood ... What was it that made him afraid to remember? He forced himself to lie still and there came to him a recollection of a tormented night: he'd been ill in bed and his mother had told him to go to sleep, that she was going out . . . He'd begged, wept, his teary eyes intent upon the fat, bald man who stood at his mother's side. He'd hated that man. His mother had been powdered, rouged, wearing a wide hat . . . Whom had he hated more? His mother or the man? They'd gone out and he, burning with fever, had gotten out of bed and had gone to the window and had yelled and yelled . . . His mother had told him that she'd found him the next morning lying huddled under the window, dopey with fever. He'd had pneumonia and his mother had nursed him and he'd wanted to remain ill all of his life to keep her with him. But after he'd gotten well she'd gone off again, as always, and he'd been left alone in the house all day and night, hating her, trying to think of the many things he wanted to do to her to make her feel it . . .

Full of sullen, impotent rage, he had let his heated imagination range wild and had choked back his yen to act. He'd developed into a too-quiet child who kept to himself, ignoring a world that offended him and wounded his sense of pride in what he loved most; his mother . . . He'd sought refuge in dreams of growing up and getting a job and taking his mother into some far-off land where there'd be no one to remember what had happened.

Then one cold winter day—he was eight years old—his mother had been hauled off to jail as a public nuisance and Aunt Tillie had come down from New York and fetched him. He'd never learned the name of his mother's offense; when he'd asked Aunt Tillie about it, she'd shaken her head and turned him off with: "It's the men who ruin women, Erskine."

But he knew in his heart that whatever it was the men had done, his mother had been a willing accomplice, had laughed and had had a good time while doing it.

His mother had remained in prison for two years and, a year after her release, she died. He recalled how Aunt Tillie had wept, for they had not had enough money to make the trip to Atlanta. Uncle Ted had attended to everything and had written him a long letter—he had lost that letter!—which had said: "Your poor mother who loved you has passed on . . ."

He'd not wept; he'd just been stunned, surprised, and relieved. He knew that he'd been long waiting to hear that she was no more and, when he heard it, he'd felt so guilty that he'd been ill in bed for a week . . . From that time on he felt that he had something to live down, to overcome.

He stirred on his bed, his eyes wide open, staring. Well, he'd overcome it, hadn't he? He'd conquered that dark, shameful episode, had come through. His life no longer touched the dark, strange, twisted actions of his mother or his own agonized past reactions to her.

Tony's drum assailed his ears again. Yes; he'd get up. This was Minnie's day off and he'd put on a pot of coffee. I'll even have time to review my Sunday School lesson. . . .

He pulled from bed and lifted his six feet to full height; he yawned and rubbed his eyes with the backs of his hands. He stripped off his pajamas and loomed naked, his chest covered with a matting of black hair, his genitals all but obscured by a dark forest, his legs rendered spiderlike by their hirsute coating. Tufts of black hair protruded even from under his arms. Nude, Erskine looked anything but pious or Christian. He pulled on his robe and lumbered into the kitchen and filled the coffee pot, lit the flame of the gas stove, listening to Tony's shouting:

"Bang! Bang! Bang! You're dead!"

He sighed. If only he could take that child to Sunday School! As twigs are bent, so grow the trees ... Twice he'd shyly asked Mrs. Blake's permission to take Tony to Sunday School and she'd consented, but each Sunday morning when he'd been ready to go, she'd been sleeping and Tony had not been properly dressed. Too much nightclubbing, too much whiskey, and God knows what else ... His nose wrinkled in disgust as he doffed his robe and entered the bathroom. He adjusted the hot and cold water faucets until the twin streams ran tepid. He was about to take off his wrist watch preparatory to stepping under the shower when his doorbell shrilled.

"Who is it?" he called, turning and standing in the bathroom door, his right hand lifted to reach for his robe.

"Paper boy!" an adolescent voice called. "Wanna collect this morning, please!"

"Oh, yes. Just a moment," he answered.

He'd promised to pay that boy this morning but, gosh, he'd forgot to get change. Still nude, he crossed the room and put his mouth to the door panel and called out:

"Say, will next week be all right? Really, I've no change; I'm sorry ... Or do you want to take down a twenty-dollar bill and get some—?"

"See you next week, Mister!" the boy called to him. "You owe me two-twenty; that right?"

"That's right," he told the boy.

He heard the thud of his thick Sunday paper hit the carpeted floor of the hallway outside and then the muffled sound of swift feet rushing toward the elevator; he caught the clank of the elevator door opening and closing ... Yes; he'd have to remember and pay that paper boy next Sunday; it wasn't right to keep a kid like that waiting for his money ... He might have need of it ...

Then he heard his coffee pot boil over in the kitchen. Golly! He'd made that flame too high! Still nude, he sprinted into the kitchen and lowered the gas fire. The redolence of coffee roused his hunger; he opened the refrigerator and hauled out the eggs, the butter, the bacon, a jar of strawberry jam, and a tin of chilled fruit juice. Padding on bare feet, he visualized the plate of succulent food he'd have.

About to reenter the bathroom, he paused. Better get my paper ... Two weeks ago his Sunday paper had been stolen. Secreting his naked body, he cracked the door and peered to left and right in the sunlit hallway. Nobody's there ... Half of the bulk of his Sunday paper lay near his toes, but the other half, evidently having slid, was scattered at the foot of the stairway. Feeling a draft of air on the skin of his unclothed body, he stooped and gathered the wad of papers at his feet, his left hand holding open the door behind him. Why did that boy fling his paper about like this? Mad maybe because I didn't pay 'im ...

He pushed the door back into his room and waited to see if it would remain open. He saw it swinging to, towards him, slowly. He'd have to open the door wide, all the way back to the wall; and, in that way, he'd have time enough to grab the other section of the paper and get back to his door before it closed. Pushing his door all the way back until it collided with the wall of the room, he watched it; it was still. He sprang nudely forward in the brightly-lighted hallway and, with a sweep of his right hand, scooped up the second half of his paper, pivoted on his bare heels, and was about to rush forward to reenter his apartment when the door began to veer slowly to, towards him. With his left hand outstretched, he dashed toward the door and reached the sill just as the door, pushed by a strong current of air, slammed shut with a thunderous metallic bang in his face. He blinked, quickly seized hold of the doorknob with his right hand and rattled it firmly. The door did not budge; it was locked!

He frowned, staring, a look of mute protest in his eyes. He became dismayingly conscious of his nudity; a sense of hot panic flooded him; he felt as though a huge x-ray eye was glaring into his very soul; and in the same instant he felt that he had shrunk in size, had become something small, shameful . . . With flexed lips he rattled the knob of the door brutally; the door still held. He knew that his door was locked, but he felt, irrationally, that it would just *have* to open and admit him before anyone saw him here nude in the hallway . . . Then his lips parted in comprehension as he remembered that only last month he had had the lock on the door changed, had installed a new system of steel bolts. There had been a series of robberies in the building and he had taken that precaution to protect himself. Now, even if he hurled his whole weight of two hundred pounds against it, that door would stand fast . . .

"Oh, God," he breathed.

Again he clutched the knob of his door and shook it with fury, looking with dread over his shoulder as he did so, fearing that someone might come into the hallway. The door remained secure, solid, burglarproof. He glanced down at his hairy legs, his frizzled chest; save for the clumsy hunk of the Sunday edition of the *New York Times,* he was nude, frightfully nude.

Erskine's moral conditioning leaped to the fore, lava-like; there flashed into his mind an image of Mrs. Blake who lived in the apartment next to his, the door that was but six inches from his right hand; also there rose up before his shocked eyes the prim face of Miss Brownell, a faded, graying spinster of forty-odd, who lived just across the hall from him; and he saw, as though staring up into the stern face of a judge in a courtroom, the gray, respectable faces of Mr. and Mrs. Fenley—Fenley of the Chase National Bank!—who lived in the apartment which was just to the left of the elevator. Good God! He was superintendent of the Mount Ararat Sunday School; he was a consulting advisor to the Longevity Life Insurance Company; he had a bank balance of over forty thousand dollars in cash; he had more than one hundred thousand dollars in solid securities, including government bonds; he was a member of Rotary; a thirty-second degree Mason; and here he was standing nude, with a foolish expression on his face, before the locked door of his apartment on a Sunday morning ...

A fine film of sweat broke out over the skin of his face. Again he grasped the doorknob and strained at it, hoping that his sheer passion for modesty would somehow twist those cold bolts of steel; but the door held and he knew that steel was steel and would not bend. There was no doubt about it; he was locked out, locked out naked in the hallway and at any second one of his neighbors' doors would open and someone would walk out and find him ... They'd scream, maybe, if they were women. Good God, what could he do? His face was wet with sweat now.

He tensed as the faint sound of the elevator door opening downstairs came to him, echoing hollowly up the elevator shaft. Somebody was coming up! Maybe to this floor! He glared about in the sun-flooded hallway, searching for nooks and crannies in which to hide, clutching awkwardly his bundle of Sunday papers. His hairy body, as he glanced down at it, seemed huge and repulsive, like that of a giant; but, when he looked off, his body felt puny, shriveled, like that of a dwarf. And the hallway in which he stood was white, smooth, modern; it held no Gothic recesses, no Victorian curves, no Byzantine incrustations in, or behind which, he could hide.

The elevator was coming up . . . He felt that he was in the spell of a dream; he wanted to shake his head, blink his eyes and rid himself of this nightmare. But he remained hairy, nude, trembling in the morning sun. If that was Miss Brownell coming up, she might scream; she'd surely complain, maybe to the police . . . He felt dizzy and his vision blurred. The muted hum of the rising elevator came nearer. Where could he hide himself? He prayed that whoever was coming up in the elevator was not getting off at this floor. Flattening his back against the cold, wooden panels of his door, pressing the bunch of newspapers tight-ly against his middle, he closed his eyes, reverting for a moment to the primitive feelings that children have—reasoning that if he shut his eyes he would not be seen. The muscles of his legs quivered and sweat broke out in the matted hair of his chest. He heard the elevator pass his floor and keep on rising . . . Thank God!

He relaxed, swallowed; then, gritting his teeth till they ached, he whirled and rattled his doorknob again, knowing that the door would not open, but rattling the knob because he *had* to do *something* . . .

Whom could he call for help? But if he called out, somebody was sure to open a door and he could not control who it would be ... God ... He felt like vomiting and, on top of it all, through the locked and bolted door, he heard his coffee pot boiling over again.

He stiffened, hearing the telephone ring in Miss Brownell's apartment. *What could he do?* The sound of a distant door opening and closing came to him, then he heard the far-off music of a radio. It was getting late; the morning was passing; each second brought discovery closer. Despair made him feel weak as he heard the elevator descending and a minute later he heard the elevator door opening and closing downstairs. Then the soft, low whine of the elevator wafted up; it was climbing towards him once more ... Lord ... Once more he stood with his back glued to the panels of the door, shielding himself with the newspapers, his body as still as a tree, sweat dripping from his chin. The drone of the elevator came nearer; it reached the tenth floor and passed, going upward again. He sighed.

He had to do something, but what? He wanted to run, but fought off the urge, fearing that any move he made would worsen his predicament. Hell, he breathed, giving vent to a curse for the first time in many long years.

Oh, he had an idea! Yes; that's what he'd do ... If he got into the elevator and rode down to the first floor, he could conceal himself in the elevator and call to Westerman, the building superintendent. Yes, that was his only chance ... What a foolish, wild, idiotic thing to do—trapping one's self naked in a building in broad daylight! Get hold of that superintendent; that was the thing ... The superintendent had a passkey for every apartment in the building.

He crept on the tips of his toes to the elevator, holding the Sunday newspaper in front of him, feeling that perhaps even the inert metal of the elevator machinery would scorn his nakedness and refuse to obey. But, when he did push the button, the elevator responded and he could hear the dull purr of the electric motor and could see, through the dim square of glass set high in the elevator door, the wobbly steel cables lifting the cage of the elevator upwards, towards him. He kept his eyes on the shut doors of other apartments. God, if only he could get hold of that superintendent...

The elevator finally arrived. He squinted through the door's dark rectangle of glass; it was empty... He yanked open the door and stepped inside, feeling lost and foolish to be entering an elevator naked like this. He had the sensation of being transparent; he felt vaguely that he had had this same experience somewhere and at some time before in his life. He pushed the button for the first floor and his body shook from the sudden descent of the elevator. God, if he had only five minutes of grace before anyone showed up!

He looked at his watch; it was only eight o'clock, yet he felt that he'd been dodging naked like this for hours... Down; down; down; the elevator moved so slowly that he felt that it would take an eternity to get to the bottom. When he looked at the newspapers that he was crushing against his body, he saw that they showed dark and gray where his sweat, dripping from his chin, was dampening them.

The elevator stopped with a soft bounce at the first floor; he peeped through the cloudy square of glass and saw two laughing young girls, seemingly in their late teens, about to open the door. He sprang and grabbed the door with his right hand and, hugging the newspapers with his left elbow, reached with his left hand, not daring to breathe, and pushed the button for the tenth floor. At once the elevator started up again and he let his breath expire through parted lips. Yes; he'd have to get out of this elevator; it was too dangerous . . .

But how could he get back into his apartment? The elevator buzzer rang in his ears and he shivered; somebody was ringing for the elevator . . . ! He kept his teeth clamped and something seemed to be jumping in his stomach, like a nerve cut loose from his ganglion, writhing. He brushed rivulets of water from his forehead, bit his lips, waited, counting the floors: seventh, eighth, ninth, tenth . . . The elevator halted; he reached forward to open the door, but paused and stared through the murky block of glass to see if the hallway was empty. Then, just as he was about to open the door, the elevator started again, going *downward!*

He searched frantically for the red emergency button, found it, jammed it fumblingly with the forefinger of his right hand; the elevator stopped. He wanted to scream and bring this spell of unreality to an end; but this unreality was real; he was experiencing this . . . Now, the button for the tenth floor. He reached out to push it, but, before his finger touched it, the elevator was climbing *upward!* A chorus of buzzings was now sounding in his ears; many people were calling for the elevator . . . For a moment he stood paralyzed, realizing that now a backlog of tenants was waiting on several floors, all trying to get possession of the elevator.

He had to stop the elevator, but his overanxiousness warped his judgment and made him lose time. It seemed that he had to look longer than ordinarily to find the right button to push. Again he leaped upon the red emergency button and hit it and the elevator jolted to a halt. His eyes darted and found the button for the tenth floor; he extended his hand to push it, and, before he could touch it, the elevator moved, going *down* once more.

He groaned. A desire to do nothing to save himself shot through him. But he couldn't act like that... Again he pounced on the red emergency button and rammed it with his finger, but his hand was trembling so that when he tried to punch the button for the tenth floor, he pushed, by mistake, the one for the fifteenth floor. Damn! Obediently, the elevator was lifting upward. Once more he shoved the red button; the elevator stopped dead, shaking him. He was now between the eleventh and twelfth floors. And, before he could touch the button for the tenth floor, the elevator dropped downward, taking his naked body—dripping as though he were in a Turkish bath—to the first floor where those two young girls were undoubtedly still waiting...

Stupidly, he stared at the rows of buttons. Once again he broke the elevator's descent by pressing the red button again and quickly indented the button for the tenth floor, and the elevator went into action *too* quickly, so quickly that he was not certain if *he* or someone *else* had pressed the button, if *he* or someone *else* had put the elevator into action. In suspense he watched the floors pass. He couldn't stand it; he had to know *who* had set the elevator into motion... He stopped the machinery again and, with a dart of his finger that was like the lick of a serpent's tongue, he flicked the button for the tenth floor; the elevator sank, even and smooth in its glide. The elevator stopped at the tenth floor, *his* floor.

His knees were bent with tension. Then he sucked

in his breath. Through the dingy plate of glass he saw Miss Brownell standing there, her hand stretched out to enter the elevator. A growl rose in his throat and he flung himself against the door. *What could he do?*

Yes; he had to get to the eleventh floor where the hallway was empty, and leave the elevator! And he'd hide on the stairway until Miss Brownell had gone. He pushed the button for the eleventh floor and the elevator lifted upward and he knew that it was *he* who commanded the elevator to move this time. There was now a loud banging on the elevator doors . . .

"What's the matter?"

"Send that elevator down!" a man's voice boomed.

"Wait, will you?" Erskine screamed, his body shaking with rage, shame, despair, and a sickness which he could not name.

The elevator came to a standstill at the eleventh floor and, through the cloudy square of glass, he saw his way clear. He opened the door and stepped out, feeling that he was escaping an enormous throng of encircling, hostile people armed with long, sharp knives, intent upon chopping off his arms, his legs, his genitals, his head . . . Squeezing the wet wad of newspapers close to his drenched skin, he crept down the stairway, leaving dark tracks of water each time his naked feet touched the purplish carpet. His body was so hot that the warm air of the hallway seemed, by contrast, cold. The sunlit hall was quiet save for muffled sounds of radios coming from surrounding apartments.

He heard the elevator going down. Hugging the cold, marble wall, he descended. There . . . He could see a tip of Miss Brownell's wide hat and a stretch of her white dress as she waited for the elevator.

He clung to the wall and tried to master his breathing. Finally he saw Miss Brownell's white hand reach for the handle of the elevator door; the door opened; she stepped inside; now, at last, the hallway on his floor was free... So long had he waited for this respite that he now, quite foolishly, felt that he had almost solved his problem. He ran to the door of his apartment and, knowing that it was locked, rattled the knob once again, hearing the elevator settling downstairs on the first floor. He heard the door opening and closing; then the sound of the elevator moving into motion again floated to him.

His eyes glistened and he stared about crazily. *What could he do?* Then his lips opened in surprise. YES, THERE WAS HIS BATHROOM WINDOW WHICH WAS KEPT OPEN ALWAYS A FEW INCHES AND HE COULD MAYBE CLIMB INTO IT FROM THE BALCONY THAT WAS JUST BENEATH THAT WINDOW... Maybe he could get into his apartment that way...? He'd be publicly exposed on the balcony for a few seconds, but that was better than this terror... It was worth trying. He should have thought of it earlier. Now, maybe he had a chance, if only that door leading to the balcony was unlocked.

He sketched out his plan of action, visualizing each move, listening with dread to the drone of the machinery as it lifted the elevator... *God, it was stopping at this floor...!*

Springing into action, he dropped the newspapers, bolted down the hallway and veered for the door as fast as his naked feet could skim across the carpet. In one vicious, sweeping movement, he seized hold of the knob of the door and yanked violently at it and felt it opening in his wet hand. He was fronting a brightly lighted balcony and his eyes were staring

straight into the full morning sun and he was blinded
for a moment. His momentum now carried him out
upon the balcony and he was turning his naked
body in the direction of the window of his bathroom even before he saw where he was going.

His right leg encountered some strange object and
he went tumbling forward on his face, his long,
hairy arms flaying the air rapaciously, like the paws
of a huge beast clutching for something to devour,
to rend to pieces . . . He steadied himself partially by
clawing at the brick wall and then he saw, in one
swift, sweeping glance, little Tony's tricycle over
which he had tripped and fallen and also there
flashed before his stunned eyes a quick image of
Manhattan's far-flung skyline in a white burst of
vision and also, like a crashing blow against his skull,
Tony, his little white face registering shock, staring
at him, clad in a cowboy's outfit, standing atop his
electric hobbyhorse near the edge of the balcony, his
slight, frail body outlined, like an image cut from a
colored cardboard, against a blue immensity of hori-
zon . . .

The physical force that had carried him through
the doorway now propelled him towards little Tony
who was holding a toy pistol gripped in his right
hand . . . Erskine checked himself in his blind rush;
his naked foot slipped on the concrete and he fell
against the top railing encircling the balcony, feeling
it shake, sway, and wobble as his two hundred
pounds struck it. He was lying now with one of his
shoulders resting against the railing . . . Tony, poised
atop the electric hobby-horse, opened his mouth to
scream and then, slowly—it seemed to Erskine's
imagination when he thought of it afterwards that
the child had been floating in air—little Tony fell
backwards and uttered one word:

"Naaaaaw . . . !"

The child went backwards, toward the void yawn-
ing beyond the edge of the balcony, his left hand
lashing out, clutching for something to grab hold of,
to hold onto, and his right hand still gripping the
toy pistol. Erskine sensed that Tony was trying to
seize hold of the top iron railing that encircled the
balcony; and, as he struggled to say something, to
yell a warning, to move, he saw little Tony fall onto
the top iron railing and for a split second the child
was poised there. The electric hobbyhorse had also
fallen against the iron railing which still trembled
under Erskine's shoulder. In the glare of golden sun
the tableau was frozen for a moment, with Tony
staring at Erskine with eyes of horror. Erskine's hand
reached hesitantly towards Tony and Tony's little
body convulsed with panic. Erskine's hand dropped;
he felt that Tony feared him . . . Tony! he screamed
without words and wanted to take hold of the child's
leg, but he was afraid to move. Then, impulsively, he
stretched out his arms toward Tony and Tony's little
left hand groped flutteringly for the top iron railing;
he actually saw Tony's tiny fingers close over the
iron railing and then the railing began to sag and
bend under the combined weight of Erskine's body,
Tony's body, and the electric hobbyhorse; the railing gave way . . . Erskine saw a brick come loose from
the wall and Tony went from sight, plunging downward, the fingers of his left hand loosening about the
iron railing and finally leaving it; Tony was gone
downward, down ten floors to the street below . . .

"Tony," Erskine sang out in a low moan.

Then he was still, nude, dripping wet, not breathing, his senses refusing to acknowledge what had
happened all too clearly before his eyes. Tony had
fallen off the balcony! No; no . . . ! *He'd be killed . . . !*

He forgot that he was naked and stood staring at
the loosened iron railing, his hands lifted in midair,
the fingers curved and turned inward toward his
hirsute body that gleamed wetly in the brilliant sunlight. Then he moved slowly and hesitantly toward
the iron railing which now dangled loose and protruded over the side of the balcony. He wanted to
look down there, but the mere thought made him
dizzy ... Mechanically, he glanced at his bathroom
window. He was straining his ears, waiting to hear
some sound—a sound that he thought would surely
stop the beating of his heart. Then he heard it; there
came a distant, definite, soft, crushing yet pulpy:
PLOP!

A spasm went through his body; he covered his
face with his hands; he knew that Tony's body had
at last hit the black pavement far below; it seemed
that he had been standing here naked on this balcony in the hot morning's sun waiting for an eternity
to hear that awful sound, a sound that would re-
verberate down all the long corridors of his years in
this world, a sound that would follow him, like a
taunting echo, even unto his grave ...

Erskine groped for the support of the wall behind
him, feeling that some invisible power had numbed
his body. He suppressed an impulse to weep and
tried to understand what had happened. But the
event he had witnessed, the horror in which he
had somehow participated contained so many shad-
owy elements that he was baffled. Had Tony fallen
because he had been afraid of him, or had that balcony railing simply given way, or what? He stared
at the iron railing, then looked about, as though
seeking another presence. Finally the reality of it
came to him clearly: Tony had been so frightened of

his wet, hairy body, of his distorted, sweating face, of his brutal rushing to the balcony that he had lost his balance, had tilted on the railing, and had plummeted ... His skull tightened as he pictured, in spite of himself, Tony's little smashed and bloody body lying on the concrete pavement below, perhaps quivering still ... *He'd scared that poor child* ... He hadn't intended to; but they would say that he had done it on purpose ... ? GOD! NO! He'd tell 'em what had happened ... No one could possibly blame him, could they? But, if no one had seen him on that balcony, then why tell ... ? What good could telling do now? Tony was no doubt dead and it was too late to help him ... And, if he *did* tell, what *could* he tell ... ? That he'd been trapped naked and had run upon the balcony to climb into the window of his bathroom and had so terrified the child that he had fallen? *Who'd* believe that?

He was still nude; he had to hide ... The yellow sun rekindled his terror. His bathroom window was some three feet above him ... Tiptoeing, he found that his fingers were inches short of the ledge. Yes; regardless of what had happened to Tony, he had to seek shelter for his nakedness. That infernal electric hobbyhorse! That fool contraption from which Tony had fallen ... Maybe, if he stood upon it, he could reach the ledge of his window? He'd try. He placed the hobbyhorse beneath the window, stepped upon it, feeling it swaying a bit, and grabbed hold of the ledge of his bathroom window. He felt dizzy as his naked body dangled perilously in air; the hobbyhorse slid from beneath his feet and clattered metallically over on its side. He clung to the ledge with both hands, flexed his muscles, hoisted himself upward with a lunge and pushed the resisting window up a little, feeling something hot and sharp biting into the flesh of his left palm. Suspending his weight on his right hand, he took his left hand from the ledge and glanced at it out of the corner of his eye: a deep, bloody gash extended from his thumb across the top of his hand ... Already blood was seeping in a red line down his arm ... He had to work fast; shoving strainingly with his wounded hand against the window, he slid it up ... Yes; now he could make it. Skinning his knees and elbows, panting, he struggled his slippery body up and went head first through the window and fell upon the commode, rolled over and lay still, gasping for breath, relaxing ... He was saved ...

His rioting impulses slowly grew somewhat quiet. His damp nude body lay huddled on the tiled bathroom floor, his head inclining weakly against the porcelain side of the tub. The soft, pelting drone of water against the shower curtain made him recall that he'd been about to bathe—it was like summoning up something out of the remote past. He became aware of his smarting, bleeding knees which were now doubled under him, and then a wild pain made him suck in his breath; his left palm was throbbing in agony. He inspected the livid gash from which blood was oozing with each beat of his heart. His eyes blinked slowly. *What had happened?* For a second he yearned to perform a mental act and annul it all; but no, he couldn't; it had happened; it was real, as real as that red blood running out of his left hand ...

He pulled himself up and went to the sink and let cold water flow over the wound. Pinching the flesh together, he held the wound closed with the firm but soft pressure of the tips of his fingers. He looked around, dazed. God, there was blood on the window sill ... He grabbed a towel with his right hand, dampened it under the faucet and swabbed the

bloody spots away from the sill and the floor. He
rinsed the towel clear of stains and left it balled in
the sink.

Tony's dead! He began to tremble and he leaned
weakly upon the edge of the bathtub. Good God!
What could he do? Tentatively, he lifted the pressure of his fingers from his left palm and at once the
blood began to flow again. He'd have to hold the
wound shut until the blood had coagulated...

Automatically, his mind sought for someone else
upon whom to shunt the blame for what had happened; but, remembering the undeniably accidental nature of the episode, he realized that he didn't
need a scapegoat upon which to dump the responsibility. It had all transpired so quickly, so inevitably,
so utterly shorn of any intention on his part that he
could have sworn that it had happened to somebody else.

The incident had thrust him entirely on his own,
and nothing he had ever heard of could offer him
any guidance now. Clinging to the whole balcony
tableau of horror was a hopeless nebulosity, something irresistibly unreal; one moment he felt that
he knew exactly what had happened, and yet the
next moment he was not so sure. His jaws trembled
as he heard again that distant, unmistakably cushy:
PLOP! Dread rammed a hot fist down his throat as
he wondered if anyone had seen him naked on that
balcony... *Christ*... Maybe somebody was now
phoning the police that a naked man had been seen
chasing a child! Under the sweat of his face his
skin turned gray. What could he do? Tell his story
now, at once? He bowed his head in indecision. But
maybe nobody had seen him and if he started babbling now he would only put a frightful idea in other
people's minds. Perhaps he should say nothing...?

He stood and stared again at the opened bathroom

window. Yes; he ought to have steeled himself and
looked down into the street to see where Tony had
fallen. A new idea made him feel that he too was
hurtling through space. Suppose, in falling, Tony
had managed to catch hold of an iron railing jutting
out, had checked the velocity of his descent, had
cushioned his fall so that he was now hurt, but
alive—? Then Tony would tell how he had come
rushing, naked and wild-eyed, out upon that balcony . . .

A lightning wish seized him; it was a wish that
Tony was dead, that Tony had fallen all the way to
the street without touching anything, that Tony had
died instantly upon his impact with the pavement.
Guilt and shame filled him, yet that wish persisted.

He wanted to look through the half-opened window and see if people were looking in his direction,
but he had the sensation that some invisible presence was watching him; he felt that looking out of
that window supplied proof of a guilt of some kind
. . . His mind was now working rapidly. *The window
of Mrs. Blake's kitchen looked out toward his balcony!* Good Lord . . . Maybe she'd seen it all, and
was too stunned, too stricken to weep or scream . . . ?
He shook his head. The truth was that Mrs. Blake
was probably sleeping off a night of high-powered
drinking and carousing . . . He hoped that she was.

He moved to the window, placed his bare feet
astride the commode and squinted at an array of
shut windows; all was quiet, still. Quickly he shut
the window and walked like a drunken man into
the kitchen where a cloud of vapor was spouting
from the coffee pot and fogging the windowpanes.
He turned out the gas; then, mechanically, using
his right hand, he replaced the eggs, bacon, butter,
jam, and the tin of fruit juice back into the refrigera-

tor and softly closed the door. His appetite was
gone ...

Still nude, he wandered back into his bedroom and
saw his bathrobe lying crumpled on a chair; he
snatched it up and struggled into it. His neglecting
to put on that robe was the cause of it all ... Tears
formed in his eyes; he nursed his bruises, feeling
that there was something urgent he had to do. The
faint wail of a police siren sounded through the Sunday morning calm and his body jerked. Had someone
seen Tony's little body falling, or had someone come
across it in the street and phoned the police?

Erskine wilted. Maybe he'd be arrested in a matter
of minutes ... He'd been urgently wanting to go to
his bedroom window and peer down into the street
to see where Tony had fallen, but sheer terror had
kept the desire out of his consciousness. He took a
step toward the window, then paused. Wouldn't
somebody see him staring down into that street and
couldn't it be said later that *that* was proof that he
already knew what had happened?

He shook his head. No; he would look out of the
window because he'd heard the sirens howling; and
that howling was now rising to a scream that was
coming nearer and nearer. He stanched the flow of
sweat on his brow by wiping his forehead with the
sleeve of his bathrobe. The sun's heat was now
spreading in the room, filling the air. If anyone
questioned him about Tony, he must not let himself
be caught off guard and blurt out something that
would entangle him in a bog of contradictions. In
his insurance work he had dealt with criminals
enough to know that to be caught in even a trivial lie
might lead to complications. For example, if he'd
known that Tony had fallen and had made no out-
cry, would that not imply that he possessed a guilty

knowledge of a deeper nature than what had actually happened? Just what, then, would his story be?
But wasn't this question idle, premature as long as
he didn't know if Tony was dead or alive? He had
first to determine what the facts were.

Yes; everything hinged upon a dead Tony that
would leave him free to invent any story he liked, or
remain silent, whichever course suited him more. In
his tortured cogitations, Erskine felt that it was
imperative to separate two distinct sets of facts: his
running half-crazed and naked upon that balcony
was one thing; his seeing Tony fall and his inability
to save him was another thing. And his consciousness
protested violently the putting of the two of them in
any way together for, when associated in his feelings, these compounded events swamped him with a
sense of guilt that was deeper than that contained
in the accident which his panic had brought about.

At last he went to the window and tried to see
down into the street, but he was much too far away
to make out anything save a patch of pavement on
the opposite side. He leaned out cautiously now and
stared down and at once he saw a small black knot
of people gathered directly below him on the sidewalk near the curb, forming a circle about something
which he could not see. Yes, that must be the body of
Tony they were gaping at ... More sirens were
screeching now; a moment later a police car tore
around the corner and pulled to a stop athwart the
throng of people.

Without knowing it, Erskine covered his mouth
with his right palm. His fate was down there where
those people stood; he stifled an impulse to rush
down and join the crowd. What if Tony was still
alive? He'd read in newspapers about how relaxed
children were when they fell, that children had been

known to fall six floors and still live ... And if Tony was alive, what would he say? He leaned weakly against the window casing, hearing Tony's piping voice telling the police that he'd been playing alone upon the balcony and then Mr. Fowler had come running, panting, wild-eyed, naked, and angry upon him and he had been so frightened that he'd fallen ...

And what would be his rebuttal to Tony's story? Could he tell the police that he'd tried to get his paper and that his door had slammed shut and he'd been trapped in the hallway and had been dodging naked and terrorized through the building and had finally rushed to the balcony like that ... ? Erskine knew instinctively how others would regard that story and his knowing made even *him* protest against believing it. And if he didn't believe it, would others? Yet it was an objectively true story; it had happened just like that ...

Such a story would be the ruin of him. What would the *Daily News* or the *Mirror* think of it? What would his friends and relatives think? They'd think that he was "queer" ... As the word *queer* came to his mind, he felt again a tight cap of something like steel pressing down upon his skull and he all but collapsed. Yes; these days everybody was talking about "complexes" and the "unconscious"; and a man called Freud (which always reminded him of *fraud!*) was making people believe that the most fantastic things could happen to people's feelings. Why, they'd say that he'd gone *deliberately* onto that balcony like that, nude ...

He saw Westerman, the building superintendent whom he had sought so futilely and frantically half an hour ago, running toward the crowd, pulling on his coat. Another police car arrived, its siren scream-

ing and its brakes whining as it came to a halt beside the crowd. Policemen poured out of it. An am-
bulance came. Erskine lifted his eyes and scanned
the other windows of the apartment building;
no one had as yet looked out. Again his vision
plunged down and he saw the policemen driving the
crowd back. Ah, there was little Tony . . . A tiny,
dark, oblong object, like a broken doll, sprawled in
the midst of a vast pool of blood . . . The body lay
half on the curb and half on the sidewalk, about
five feet from a fire hydrant.

"*He's dead,*" he whispered with relief, then whirled
guiltily, expecting to find that someone had over-
heard him.

Suddenly he was aware of white blobs of faces in
the crowd turning upward and he shrank quickly
back into his room; he glanced at the other windows.
Yes; other people were looking down now, but no
face had turned to look at his window. He sank upon
his unmade bed; tears of remorse and relief clogged
his eyes. He whimpered:

"Oh, God, why did this have to happen to
me . . . ?"

Erskine was undone and, had there been anyone
at that moment to hear his confession, he would have
spilled out more than he knew. His life had gone
deadly wrong and, in his extremity, he was trying
to give up and find repose in some higher wisdom
that he felt vaguely was in his heart.

The dim shrill of Mrs. Blake's phone brought him
to his feet; his eyes stared as though trying to see
through the far wall of his room. He listened as the
phone pealed again and he pictured her rising sleep-
ily from bed, rubbing her eyes, struggling to overcome last night's drinking, and reaching for the

phone ... No; the phone was ringing again. In the midst of its sixth ring, it stopped abruptly. He tiptoed into the living room whose left wall formed a common partition with her bedroom, put his ear to the cool white plaster and tried to listen, but could hear nothing. Then he flinched as a scream came to his ears. Yes; she knew now ... The scream came again, then again. He heard the elevator door opening and closing in the hallway and then there came the sound of Mrs. Blake's doorbell ringing insistently, repeatedly.

Ought he to look into the hallway? He had the right to find out who was doing all that screaming, hadn't he? Composing himself, still clamping the tips of his fingers over the wound of his left palm, he went to the door, opened it and saw Westerman, the building superintendent, standing in the open doorway of Mrs. Blake's apartment, with his back to him. He could not see Mrs. Blake, but he could hear her voice:

"No; no; no ... What are you *saying?*"

Mrs. Blake pushed Westerman aside, ran out of her apartment in her nylon nightgown, and stopped in the middle of the hallway; she looked around blindly, her eyes wild and her face white with shock. She rushed on bare feet toward the balcony.

"Mrs. Blake," Westerman called helplessly to her, "he's not *there.* I tell you he *fell ...*"

Mrs. Blake paused and, without turning around, she screamed. Then she whirled and clapped her hands to her face.

"Tony," she moaned.

Westerman was staring at the crazed, half-nude woman.

"Somebody *find* Tony!" Mrs. Blake wailed.

"But Mrs. Blake . . ." Westerman began again.

The elevator door opened and Mrs. Westerman came running out.

"Oh, God, you poor woman!" she cried.

Erskine noticed that Westerman was staring about with a dull, stupid expression.

"What's happening?" Erskine asked in a whisper.

Westerman lifted his hands in a gesture of hopelessness.

"It's Tony . . . Poor little Tony," the man said.

"What about him? Is there anything wrong?" Erskine asked.

Westerman turned away, blinking, unable to speak. Mrs. Westerman now glanced toward Erskine and shook her head sadly. Mrs. Blake was struggling to break free from Mrs. Westerman, straining toward the elevator.

"Take me to Tony," she whimpered.

"Mrs. Blake," Westerman was pleading, trying to help his wife hold the woman.

Erskine could see that Westerman was a little shy about handling Mrs. Blake, for the blurred outlines of her plump, curving body were distinctly visible through her sheer nylon nightgown.

"Poor little Tony's dead!" Mrs. Westerman wailed, gulping. "He fell . . . Dear God in Heaven . . . The little thing's all crushed and bloody . . . Angels of God, help us all . . ."

"No!" Erskine found himself saying, shaking his head. He wondered if he were acting naturally enough . . .

"Mary!" Westerman called to his wife in a tone of protest. "Get her *back* into her apartment . . . She's got to put on some clothes . . . She can't go down there like *that*."

Mrs. Westerman stared, finally comprehending

what her husband meant. She grabbed the struggling
Mrs. Blake firmly in her arms.

"Darling, please ... Come back into your apartment ... You must put on something ..."

"I want my baby ... Oh, God, my little baby ...
What's happened to my child, my baaaaaaby ... ?
Toooony," she sobbed, her palms cupped and held
tremblingly before her red, weeping eyes.

Erskine watched Westerman and his wife pull the
hysterically weeping woman back into her apartment, the door of which still stood open. Across the
hallway the door of the Fenley apartment opened
and Mr. Fenley, tall, gray, clad in a bathrobe, looked
out and asked: "What's going on here?"

"Seems like something has happened to Mrs.
Blake's child," Erskine told him with raised eyebrows. He didn't know how naturally he was acting;
his manner was coming without any conscious effort
on his part.

"No," Mr. Fenley grunted; he turned abruptly
back into his apartment and a moment later reap-
peared in the doorway, adjusting his spectacles to
his eyes and peering toward the door of Mrs. Blake's
apartment. "Nothing serious is the matter, I hope."

"If what Mrs. Westerman says is true, it's awful,"
Erskine told him. "She says that Mrs. Blake's son fell
off the balcony ..."

"Good Lord," Mr. Fenley breathed, his eyes
bulging.

"Oh, Henry, what's the matter?" Mrs. Fenley's
voice called from inside the apartment.

"Something's happened to that Blake child, it
seems," Mr. Fenley turned and spoke to his wife
who was still inside the apartment. "They say he fell
from the balcony—"

"Oh, no!"

"When did this happen?" Mr. Fenley asked Erskine.

"This morning, I think..."

"This morning?" Mr. Fenley echoed.

"Presumably so," Erskine said.

Mrs. Fenley, frail, tall, clad also in her bathrobe, came to the door, her mouth open, her eyes staring at Erskine.

"Good morning," she greeted Erskine tensely. "What's all this about little Tony?"

"Good morning, Mrs. Fenley," Erskine answered her. "I don't know, really. Westerman says that Tony fell from the balcony and was killed..."

"Good God! From the balcony...?"

"Seems so. That's what they say. Westerman and his wife are now inside with Mrs. Blake—" He gestured toward the open apartment door.

Westerman came out of Mrs. Blake's apartment in time to overhear Mrs. Fenley's request for information.

"Little Tony fell from the balcony; he was crushed," he told them. "He must have been killed as soon as he hit the pavement..."

"The balcony on this floor?" Mrs. Fenley asked.

"Yes; I think so," Westerman said.

"Oh, dear! That poor little child," Mrs. Fenley moaned, clutching her throat and turning to her husband. She swung around, as though suddenly remembering her duty. "That poor woman... How she must be suffering—" She ran to the open door of Mrs. Blake's apartment and entered.

Erskine saw Fenley stoop and gather up the bulk of his Sunday paper and at once Erskine did the same. Surreptitiously, he tried to smooth out his crumpled wad... The elevator door had been left open and from it came the insistent sound of buzzing.

Westerman stepped to the elevator and closed the door.

"Is there anything we can do?" Mr. Fenley asked Westerman.

"I'm afraid not, sir," Westerman replied. He looked worried, stunned. "I want to see that balcony," he said at last, frowning.

"Then it *was* from this floor?" Mr. Fenley asked.

"I guess so," Westerman mumbled. "It was where he played most of the time. . . ."

"Goodness," Erskine breathed.

Erskine's legs were trembling. He had a hot impulse to tell Westerman right then and there what had happened for, maybe, they'd find it out sooner or later and blame him . . . for what? What could they blame him for? And if he had anything to tell, should he not have told it already? To try to tell now was awkward . . . And yet the longer he waited, the more impossible it would be to tell. And it all had too much the air of a wild dream to make sense. Yes; he'd follow Westerman and see how he reacted when he saw that loose iron railing jutting off the balcony into space . . . He pushed the lever on his lock and, as he did so, he cursed himself for having forgotten to do so earlier this morning. If he'd done that, all of this would not have happened; Tony would be alive, yelling, beating his drum . . . He walked behind Westerman, still wearing his bathrobe, holding his Sunday newspaper . . .

"But what happened?" Erskine asked Westerman.

"We don't know, sir," Westerman replied vaguely. "I always was kinda scared of that balcony. Too small for kids to play on."

"But is the child really *dead?*" Erskine asked. "Maybe they could still help him, save him . . ." Erskine swallowed; he could feel that his voice carried a note of a man not wanting to believe what he had heard.

"He's dead," Westerman told him flatly. "The cop said he was DOA—dead on arrival."

Westerman came to the open door giving onto the balcony and stood staring for a moment. Erskine, standing directly behind Westerman, had to tiptoe and peer over the man's shoulder to see the tumbled tricycle and the overturned electric hobbyhorse which now lay near the iron railing, having been pushed there by Erskine's naked feet when he had hoisted himself upward into the bathroom window. The iron railing was conspicuously loose; one end had been torn from the brick wall and was now extending out into space . . .

Erskine lifted his head and his eyes anxiously searched the window ledge for blood spots. There were none. Thank God . . . ! Only a miracle had kept that window ledge free of blood stains, and he had forgotten to inspect it until this very moment . . .

"Jeeeesus," Westerman breathed. "That railing came smack out of that wall . . . How on earth could that happen?"

Westerman advanced upon the balcony now.

"Could he have fallen against it?" Erskine asked him in a low, charged tone.

Westerman did not reply; he bent forward, got to his knees and examined the gaping hole from which the railing had come.

"God, the cement's loose; that's why the railing came out," Westerman spoke as though to himself. He then looked up to Erskine. "See?" he asked, pointing.

Erskine shuddered but kept his face straight. True, the cement had been somewhat loose, but he knew in his heart that Tony's weight and the blow dealt that

railing by the hobbyhorse would not have torn that
railing from that brick wall; it had been his added
weight of two hundred pounds—accidentally thrown
against the railing—that had made that railing sag
and give way . . .

"Yes," Erskine murmured.

Westerman got to his feet and stared about. "He
must've been playing on that horse and fell, maybe
. . . He went against that railing. That damned horse
is heavy. I've lifted it many a time to bring it out
here for Tony." Westerman lifted the horse. "Feel
this, Mr. Fowler," Westerman said to Erskine.

Erskine hesitated, then took hold of the horse and
lifted it; it weighed nearly sixty pounds.

"It's kind of heavy," Erskine allowed himself to
admit.

"You're telling me?" Westerman said scornfully.
"Why in God's name they want to make toys as big
and heavy as that, I don't know." Westerman scowled
in disgust. "If *he* had fallen against that railing
alone, it wouldn't have pulled loose; but when *he*
and that damned *horse*, the *two* of them, hit that
railing, it gave . . . Don't you think so?"

"Looks like it," Erskine said with a dry throat. He
felt that he was speaking the truth.

Cautiously, Westerman peered over the edge of
the balcony, then drew back, his eyes full of pity,
horror, and wonder.

"Makes me dizzy just to look down there," he
mumbled, sweat standing on his brow.

Erskine heard dull footsteps behind him; he
glanced round and saw Mr. Fenley, pale, concentrated, tense, advancing toward the balcony, his thin
lips hanging open and the sparse, blond and gray
hair on top of his head tossing in the wind.

"No child should be allowed to play on a balcony

as tiny as that," Mr. Fenley snapped with indigna-
tion. He turned and was about to leave when he almost collided with a uniformed policeman.

"Which of you is Mr. Westerman?" the policeman
asked.

"I am, sir," Westerman said. "This is awful—"

"Is this where he fell from?" the policeman asked.

"I guess so," Westerman mumbled. "These are
his playthings. And this was where he played all
the time—"

"Hmmnn," the policeman grunted, staring about.
"That iron railing . . . Was it always loose, like
that . . . ?"

"No, sir," Westerman replied stoutly. "That's the
first time in my life I've seen it like that." The man's
voice rang with conviction; he was frowning and
staring at the loose cement. "That railing was certainly not like that yesterday, sir. I washed windows
on this floor and I'd have seen it, if it had been."

"Who else comes out on this balcony?" the policeman asked.

"Nobody but Tony; he played here a lot," Westerman said.

"Whose window's that?" the policeman asked,
pointing to Erskine's bathroom window.

"That's my window," Erskine told him.

"Did you hear anything out here this morning?"
the policeman asked him.

"I heard the child beating his drum," Erskine said.

"Was there anybody with 'im?"

"Not that I know of."

"Did the child make any strange outcries?"

"I heard him shouting, playing—"

"But no sounds as though he was hurt or anything?"

"Nothing like that."

"Did any of you see the child this morning?"

"I did," Westerman said. "I unlocked the door and brought the horse out—"

"That balcony door... You say you unlocked it. Why?"

"Well, you see, sir," Westerman explained, "that door's locked at night, always. We've had a lot of robberies, sir. We didn't want anyone climbing into apartments through bathroom windows. I unlocked that door this morning at six, so Tony could play—"

"Was anyone on the balcony when you came out here then?"

"Absolutely not, sir. If there had been, I'd have seen them." Westerman was positive in his statement.

"And the child was playing alone?"

"His mother said he was, sir," Westerman said. "I just spoke to her. She lives in apartment 10C. She's there now..."

"Did anyone see the child fall?" the policeman asked.

Erskine's body tightened. What good would telling the truth do now? And he wasn't guilty of anything. But telling what had happened would make him seem somehow guilty... But ought he to lie? And remaining silent was lying... Suddenly he was resolved to stay clear of Tony's death, but he didn't want to lie baldly. How could he do that? He knew that, in a legal sense, he was not guilty; but to say that he'd seen the child fall meant becoming entangled in something that would harm him no end, and to no purpose. Was this not an exception to the general rule? Yet, didn't he have a sacred duty to tell the truth? To describe exactly what had happened? But if he did, if he said that he'd been naked and had frightened the child, wouldn't the idea leap into everybody's mind that he had been up to something "perverse"? Did telling the truth mean that one had to expose one's self uselessly to slander of that sort? But why was he so certain that others would think him "perverse"? Erskine's experience as an insurance man had taught him that man was a sneaking, guilty animal, always prone to excesses, to outlandish attitudes. Common sense urged him to hold his tongue, and he was positive that no motive other than that of prudence was prompting him to silence.

"I was in my apartment," Mr. Fenley explained. "I saw nothing. I heard a commotion and looked out of my door and saw Mrs. Blake crying and yelling . . ."

"I was taking in my paper when I heard Mrs. Blake scream," Erskine found words at last. "God, it's a pity—"

"You folks mustn't touch anything here," the policeman said. He went to the balcony and peered down, then to left and right.

Mr. Fenley went back into the hallway and Erskine followed him.

"It's awful," Erskine said to Mr. Fenley.

"It's that mother of his, if you ask me," Mr. Fenley said *sotto voce*. "She was sleeping, she said . . . Imagine! She ought to be whipped to let a child play out there."

"Guess you're right," Erskine found himself eagerly clutching at a scapegoat.

"And she's weeping," Mr. Fenley said in disgust. "She ought to."

Mrs. Fenley came out of Mrs. Blake's apartment, followed by Mrs. Westerman who was leading the weeping Mrs. Blake by the arm. Mrs. Blake had dressed, but her tumbling black hair spread wildly over her shoulders, half hiding her face and spilling down to her waist. The door of Mrs. Blake's apartment slammed shut and Erskine stared at it as though hypnotized, recalling how, just less than an hour ago, he had been standing naked and terrified before his own door that had slammed shut.

"Will she be able to get back in?" the policeman asked, coming forward.

"Don't bother," Mrs. Westerman said. "I've got passkeys to all the apartments in the building. I'll let her in when she comes back."

Mrs. Blake walked with difficulty, her knees sagging. She paused as she passed Erskine and stared blankly before her. Erskine imagined that, for half a second, her large, limpid, brown eyes were resting upon him. Or had they? He grew tense. He had to be careful and keep a tight hold on himself. . . .

Mrs. Fenley went to her husband's side and clutched his arm nervously, staring at Mrs. Westerman and Mrs. Blake. The two women, Westerman, and the policeman entered the elevator; the door closed and the elevator sank.

"Poor, poor woman," Mrs. Fenley murmured in awe.

"I wonder if there's anything we can do?" Erskine spoke uncertainly.

"Well, the police are taking care of everything now," Mr. Fenley said. "It's too bad . . . Come, dear." He took his wife's arm and led her into their apartment.

Erskine stood alone in the hallway, hugging his bundle of Sunday papers. Suddenly he was afraid to enter his apartment. He dreaded being alone now. When supported by the presence of the others, everything had seemed natural, his not telling had

had a normal aspect. But the moment he was alone and face to face with himself, he felt that he ought to tell. But how could he? He stood brooding, biting his lips.

The elevator door opened and Miss Brownell, her arms full of groceries, came out with wide eyes and a pale face.

"Oh, Mr. Fowler, do you know what has happened?" she demanded, running up to him.

"About little Tony? It's awful, awful . . . I can't believe it," he told her.

"What a ghastly, horrible thing!" Miss Brownell sang out as she closed her eyes. "I had to walk ten blocks to buy something for lunch, and when I passed down there I thought I'd faint when they told me that that was little Tony lying there all smashed . . . The poor little thing was all covered with a sheet or something. I couldn't even bear to look in his direction. They're taking him to the hospital now—"

"The hospital?" Erskine repeated her words. "But I thought the child was dead . . ." Had he spoken too abruptly, in too surprised a manner?

"He *is*," Miss Brownell assured him quickly. "But it seems that they take 'em to the hospital anyway. Mr. Westerman says that the Medical Examiner has to decide if the death was accidental or not. But, of course, it was . . . Just a formality, you know? Oh, things like this unnerve me no end . . . And that Mrs. Blake lost her husband in the war, you know? How did poor Tony fall?"

"Nobody seems to know," Erskine said uneasily.

"That Mrs. Blake," Miss Brownell pronounced the woman's name in a sudden, sober manner, biting her lips and shooting a meaningful glance at Erskine.

"Yes," Erskine said quietly, agreeing.

They had both passed a moral judgment upon the

mother of Tony. Her arms loaded, Miss Brownell was now trying to open her door, fumbling awkwardly with her key.

"Here; let me help you there," Erskine said, advancing.

"Oh, thank you," Miss Brownell said, surrendering her key.

Erskine unlocked her door and handed her her key.

"You're so kind," Miss Brownell murmured, smiling at him.

"Not at all," Erskine mumbled.

"I just can't seem to get that poor child out of my mind," Miss Brownell wailed.

"I know what you mean," Erskine said, nodding sympathetically. He felt sweat breaking out again over the skin of his body.

"Well, good-bye," Miss Brownell called, smiling sadly.

"Good morning, Miss Brownell," Erskine said.

Miss Brownell's door closed and Erskine turned and headed for his door. He stopped. He was staring at a copy of Mrs. Blake's *New York Times* that lay in a neat, folded heap at her door sill. And his copy of the *New York Times* was crushed under his arms, damp, crumpled . . . Yes; he'd exchange the newspapers . . . Mrs. Blake would be too upset to notice that her copy was not fresh, was damp and wadded. . . . She'd surely not read the paper today; and even if she did notice that her papers were soiled, wouldn't she think that Tony had been playing with them . . . ?

Stooping quickly, he let his paper fall softly to the carpet and then picked up her paper; he glanced round; no one was in sight. He sighed, still trembling slightly, then went back into his apartment, shut the door, and leaned weakly against it. He stifled a groan. He was feeling a terror that he had felt a long, long time ago, feeling it but not understanding it. He felt alone, abandoned in the world—abandoned and guilty. Why?

"God, it wasn't my fault." He spoke aloud in a stern, resentful, and insistent voice.

PART 2: AMBUSH

... one thing is the thought, another thing is the deed, and another thing is the idea of the deed.
 —Nietzsche's *Thus Spake Zarathustra*

... is there really such a world of difference between the wish and the deed?
 Theodor Reik's *The Unknown Murderer*

In the beginning was the deed.
 —Goethe's *Faust*

NUMBED, shaky, Erskine went to his bedroom
window and stared down into the street, feeling that
something grossly unfair had happened to him. The
crowd had dispersed and the sun lit to distinctness
the dark, irregular smudge where Tony's body had
lain in its pool of blood.

How utterly stupid it all was! With a violent reflex action he spun round, his face contorted with
rage; he smote his right fist into his left palm; then
his knees sagged from pain. He'd forgotten that he
had cut his hand. Blood began to flow again from
the wound; he went to the bathroom, washed it, and
sealed it with adhesive tape.

He sank into a chair, brooding. His mind strenu-
ously protested the potency of that accident. If only
he hadn't foolishly failed to flick the lever on his
lock; if only that lazy, good-for-nothing Mrs. Blake
had been looking after her child properly; if only
he hadn't left his bedroom window open, a draft of
air would not have pushed his door shut; if only
he'd taken time and looked on that balcony before
rushing out; if only, when he'd gone down nude in
the elevator, those two young girls hadn't been
waiting there; if only that cursed newsboy hadn't
come at that time; if only he'd gotten out of bed
the moment he'd opened his eyes, instead of lolling

and day-dreaming—none of this would have happened! But who, in the name of God, could have foreseen such a concatenation of events?

One aspect of the accident bothered him above all: why had little Tony been so frightened of him as to lose his balance when he'd come running nude onto the balcony? Tony knew him, admired him; then, why had he gone into such a panic . . . ? It's true that he'd been naked, and, when naked, Erskine knew that he was not a pleasant or poetic sight . . .

Erskine realized that a child's mind was a strange shadowland, and what seemed ordinary to adults would loom as something monstrous or fearful to Tony who had lived in a world of Indians, horses, bombing planes, soldiers, whales, and perhaps things never seen on land or sea. What, then, had Tony associated him with that seemed so fantastic, frightful? Why had the sudden sight of him—huge, hairy, sweating, panting—sent Tony reeling?

And where, in the medley of these unrehearsed episodes, did the element of his guilt lie? Was it because he'd denied any knowledge of how the child had died that he felt guilty? No. He knew that even now, if he told Mrs. Blake or the police how utterly blameless he'd been, he'd still feel guilty? Why?

Never in Erskine's life had his emotions been a problem to him; indeed, he had lived with the assumption that he had no emotions. From puberty onwards he had firmly clamped his emotions under the steel lid of work and had fastened and tightened that lid with the inviolate bolts of religious devotion. Now he felt ambushed, anchored in a sea of anxiety, because he was tremblingly conscious of all of his buried demons stirring and striving for the light of day. What did one do in situations like this? He then felt guilty of feeling guilty. . . . Ought he to seek ad-

vice? But from whom? And about what? His strong-
est impulse at this moment was not to talk about
this, to deny its existence; he felt that his telling
others about it would make him feel even more
guilty, that he was no longer master of himself, and
he was far too proud for that. . . .

Erskine could deal swiftly and competently with
the externalities of life. If something went wrong,
he called in a lawyer, an accountant, or a policeman,
and matters were righted at once. But who could
one summon when one's emotions went into a state
of rebellion? Vainly he groped for an explanation that
would enable him to deal with this. He felt tricked;
things shouldn't be like this! things were *not* like
this. Things had become temporarily snarled; soon,
however, he'd straighten them out again.

What had occurred was simple and, being an
executive, he ought to be able to arrive at a quick
solution. All right: the thing to do was to tell what
had happened. . . . Then why all this perturbation,
hesitation? Intuitively, he felt that some dark visitor,
long banished from his life, was knocking at the door
of his heart; and he didn't want to open that door
and see the strange but familiar features of that
visitor's face. But, if he didn't open that door, what
was he to do? Just listen endlessly to that hollow, re-
sounding knocking?

The honorable, Christian thing to do was to tell
the police; he had connections; he had money; he
could hire a lawyer. But, no; that was not the way
out; not at all. Considerations of personal safety were
not constraining him; he could, if worse came to
worst, bribe his way out. But, out of *what* would he
bribe his way? He wasn't guilty . . .

He had a foggy hunch that there was as yet some
nameless act that he could perform that would right

the wrong, redress the evil he had inadvertently
done. But whenever he was on the verge of thinking
of that act, of forming a clear image of it, he sweated,
trembled, and all but sank under the weight of morti-
fication and guilt. What, then, was that act? What
dark nature did it possess to evoke such distress in
him? He sat upon his bed and stared unseeingly.

He checked his watch; good God . . . He'd only
twenty minutes to get to Sunday School . . . He showered, dressed, fumbling with his clothes, still nursing his wounded hand. If any investigation got
under way, he didn't want it said that he'd, perhaps
from nervousness, remained away from church for
the first time in ten years. And he needed the sus-
taining solace of his fellow-Christians at this moment. He was convinced that in the end his faith in
God would lead him to a solution.

He got his Bible, his book of Sunday School les-
sons and stood undecided before that fateful door
that had slammed shut in his face. His stomach felt
queasy; he drank a glass of water and let himself out.
He crossed the bright, empty hallway, summoned
the elevator, and rode down and went out into the
street.

A policeman stood a few feet from the fire hydrant, near the spot where little Tony's body had
lain. The streets were filled with Sunday quietness.
He wanted to talk to the policeman, ask him what
had been the opinions of his colleagues about Tony's
accidental fall; but he recalled that most of the
crooks that he had caught, when he'd sleuthed in
the insurance business, had betrayed themselves by
talking too much. He forced himself to turn and walk
down the block.

It was too late to get his car from the garage, and
he felt much too nervous to drive anyway. He hailed

a taxi, gave the driver the address of his church, and settled back in the seat, mopping his wet face with a balled handkerchief. Now, what was his future conduct to be? Yes; as soon as church was over this morning, he'd visit Mrs. Blake and pay her his respects. But what would he say to her? And what, if anything, had been the meaning of that fixed, brief stare she had, while being supported by Mrs. Fenley and Mrs. Westerman, given him in the hallway? Or had he *imagined* that? Had anyone else noticed it? He chided himself for letting his overstrained nerves get the better of him. No one suspected anything; if they had, they'd have voiced it long before now. He'd better concentrate on his Sunday School lesson, which Tony's death had robbed him of time to study, so as to be able to perform his religious duties without betraying the turbulent state of his emotions. Well, he'd improvise; with God's help, he'd spread His Word ...

"Here you are, sir," the driver said, pulling to the curb in front of a huge white sandstone church topped by a white cross.

As he paid the driver, he heard the church bell tolling with melancholy softness through the sunny air. Compulsively touching the tips of the pencils clipped to his inner coat pocket, he strode with brisk, confident steps through loitering groups of young men and women and entered the church. A plaintive wave of hymn filled his ears:

> *Just as I am, without one plea*
> *But that Thy Blood was shed for me,*
> *And that Thou bidd'st me come to Thee*
> *O Lamb of God, I come.*
> *Just as I am, though toss'd about*
> *With many a conflict, many a doubt,*

Fightings and fears within, without,
O Lamb of God, I come.

Long lances of soft light falling from stained glass windows made delicate crisscrosses in the dim, vaulted interior of the church, and the serried rows of faces in the circular pews, arrayed one behind the other and stretching away into the shadows, closed around him like a sweet benediction. The nostalgia of the singing voices soothed his taut nerves and at once he felt better. The world seemed to be gaining in safety, solidity; this was *his* world, a world he believed in, trusted—a world he had supported all his life and which, in turn, buoyed him up with its sunlit faith from which all confusions had been forever banished by the boon of God's great grace.

At a long walnut table, placed before and below the pulpit, sat Mrs. Ira Claxton, smiling and nodding at him as always, her head crowned magically by a halo of snow-white hair; she was, bless her, filling in for him. The memory of Tony's death-plunge and his sense of guilt fled as he walked down the middle aisle, bowing from left to right, recognizing faces of friends, and he knew that they were all noticing him intently because, for the first time in ten years, he was fifteen minutes late. These were his people; they needed him and he needed them; theirs was a world in which little children did not, for wildly mysterious reasons, tumble from balconies to their deaths; in this world there were no dark, faceless strangers knocking at the doors of one's soul. . . .

He shook hands with Mrs. Claxton, his assistant; with Deacon Bradley, the treasurer; and with forty-year-old, shy Miss White, the Sunday School secretary. Mrs. Claxton leaned toward him and whispered:

"I was beginning to *wonder* ..."

"A terrible accident happened in my building this morning," he whispered to her. "I'll tell you about it later."

Mrs. Claxton's gray eyes widened in sympathetic concern as she nodded, not skipping a beat of the music or a word of the hymn.

The deep-throated, sonorous tones of the organ made him join in the hymn; he lifted his baritone voice to swell the volume of song. He was contented. He was *home* ...

The opening remarks had already been made by Mrs. Claxton and the next items were a prayer by Deacon Bradley; the reading of the minutes by Miss White; and the treasurer's report, also by Deacon Bradley. Following that, Erskine would introduce the morning's topic which, according to the Sunday School book he held in his moist fingers, read:

GOD'S ETERNAL FAMILY

A murky illustration depicted Jesus speaking to a vast crowd at the edge of which stood Mary, Jesus' mother, and her sons. Below the picture ran these verses:

ST. MATTHEW, 12: 46, 47, 48, 49, 50

46 While he yet talked to the people, behold, *his* mother and his brethren stood without, desiring to speak with him.

47 Then one said unto him, Behold, thy mother and thy brethren stand without, desiring to speak with thee.

48 But he answered and said unto him that told him, Who is my mother? and who are my brethren?

49 And he stretched forth his hand toward his disciples, and said, Behold my mother and my brethren!

50 For whosoever shall do the will of my Father which is in heaven, the same is my brother and sister, and mother.

As he sang he studied the text, seeking a clue. Wasn't this a clear call for him to regard Mrs. Blake as his sister in Christ? Perhaps God, in His infinite wisdom, had chosen him as an instrument when he had innocently caused poor little Tony to topple to his death? Yes; he'd find a way of making amends to Mrs. Blake. Perhaps he, too, was being mysteriously chastened of God . . . Since God had foreordained all, had prescribed the ends of life, why should he exert himself to act? Wilful, selfish action on his part might well be impiously presumptuous! It was now clear that to take this problem to the authorities would be foolish.

The beginnings of a tentative solution began to shape themselves in his mind. Yes; he'd talk to Mrs. Blake . . . But what would he say to her? Need he confess to her his stupid part in that abominable accident? But why, since he was not guilty of anything? God had but placed him on that balcony as a witness of a tragic misfortune, and he had to resign himself to God's will. Yes; he'd find a way to help that poor Mrs. Blake . . .

During the reading of the minutes and the secretary's report, Erskine resolved that he'd sound the note of God's universal family when he introduced the morning's text to the congregation. How fitting that Divine grace was shedding upon him the means to escape the poignant, terrible image of Tony's little white face, the tiny mouth gaping in terror, those frail

fingers clawing futilely at that sagging, iron railing!
Yes; that accident was God's own way of bringing a
lost woman to her senses; and he knew that his
judgment of Mrs. Blake was right, for hadn't she wal-
lowed shamelessly in the fleshpots of nightclubs? God
had punished her by snatching little Tony up to
Paradise—had garnered Tony home from the evil of
this world. He, Erskine, was but God's fiery rod of
anger! And on what better ground than that enclosed
by the church's four holy walls should such revela-
tions dawn in his soul? A sense of mission seized him.
Yes; God was giving him a mandate to face Mrs.
Blake and have it out with her!

When the moment came for him to expound the
religious, the philosophical, and emotional meaning of the morning's theme, he rose and spoke with
a fervor new to him and his audience was moved to
quiet wonder.

"... out of the coiling confusion and paltry acci-
dents cluttering our daily lives, we can build nothing
lasting, nothing true," he intoned. "We must follow
the Spirit and allow God to act in us as arbiter between the seductions of a deceptive world and His
everlasting claims. How reedlike we are when left to
our weak wills and debased instincts! Who, of his
own puny strength, possesses enough virtue to guide
himself through the maze of this sinful world? What
a mixture we are, we who are *in* this world but are
forbidden to be *of* it! What fearful battlegrounds are
our hearts!

"But, in the midst of this dark strife, God has not
deserted us! His gift, pointing the way to truth, has
assumed the guise of a sign that no man can possibly
overlook! What is that sign? THE FAMILY! And
with what a common-place attitude do we regard
this sublime spectacle of the family that comprises

God's mighty parable, a parable in which He has couched our lives from childhood onward! Man-made families lurch and wreck themselves on the rocks of circumstance, but one has only to lift his eyes, tear himself away from selfishness, and he sees, with the help of God, another family, God's eternal family—a family whose foundations are built of God's will and love."

Patting his damp brow with his folded handker-chief, Erskine concluded in simple but stern tones:

" 'Who is my mother? Who is my brother?' What terrible words! But what *saving* words! With one master-stroke of His sword of righteousness, God cut the chains of human slavery and made us all free, free to see mothers and sisters everywhere, free to recognize brothers in our neighbors, free to extend our claim of kinship! Christ challenges you to do as He did: Take the hand of even your loved ones and bring them into that higher, greater family which is of God! Christ likewise enjoins you to clasp hands with your neighbor, even your enemy—those who hate us and whom we hate—and lead them into that family where hate is no more, where enemies are transformed into brothers, neighbors! Christ denied His mother and His brothers, but only to make all women His mother and all men His brothers and neighbors!"

He sat, compulsively assuring himself that his colored pencils were intact. There was discreet hand-clapping, which was unusual for the decorous, middle-class members of the Mount Ararat Bap-tist Church. Mrs. Claxton leaned and whispered with admiration in her eyes:

"It was *wonderful!*"

"Mrs. Claxton," Erskine spoke on the spur of the moment, "would you be kind enough to take charge of my class this morning? I'm at loose ends. A child whom I loved deeply fell to his death from my balcony a few minutes before I left my apartment—"

"*Fell*, did you say?" she asked.

"Yes. Ten floors."

Mrs. Claxton's right hand flew to her mouth and her eyes rounded with shock.

"Oh, dear God!" she breathed.

"He was only five years old. It shook me, I tell you—"

"Did you know him well?"

"He was a little friend of mine."

"That's why you looked so *pale* when you came in!"

"Did I? I didn't know—"

"The moment I saw your face, I *knew* that something had happened."

"I was stunned," he mumbled, wiping his brow.

"Wasn't the child properly looked after?"

"His mother was sleeping ... She'd been out night-clubbing."

Dismay made Mrs. Claxton's fingers flutter.

"The times we live in," she sighed. "*Now* I know what made you speak so eloquently this morning.... Of course, Mr. Fowler, I'll teach your class. But I'm not nearly as good as you are. I'll do my best."

"You're a good teacher," Erskine told her. "And you're kind."

The congregation had risen and was forming itself into groups based on age and profession. Erskine's class was composed of business and professional men and women. He was grateful that Mrs. Claxton was standing-in for him and he listened to her slightly quavering voice, but his real attention was elsewhere; his consciousness was seduced by the persistent image of Mrs. Blake's nude, voluptuously sinful body which he had glimpsed twice through his open window ...

After Sunday School had let out, Erskine took Mrs. Claxton's hand in his own and implored her:

"Please, tell Reverend Barlow that I shan't be at the afternoon or evening services."

"You don't feel well, do you?" she asked compassionately.

"Really, I don't."

"We'll miss you," she told him.

Though the distance was more than fourteen blocks, he decided to walk home. But the moment he was on the hot sidewalk, under the noonday sun, amid the passers-by, his mood of confident righteousness began to ebb. *Had anyone seen him on that balcony?* Had the Medical Examiner or the police found any clues that would make them suspect that someone had been *with* Tony on that balcony? Maybe the police were waiting to question him now ... God! He suddenly didn't want to go home. And Mrs. Blake, what could he tell her? He'd offer her his condolences; but after that, what? Where was that neat solution that he'd been hugging to his heart back there in that dim, song-filled church? He *must* talk to somebody about this ... No; he *couldn't!* His steps slowed. There was but one way out for his conscience; he had to see Mrs. Blake and settle this thing ... But something in him warned him off from her.

He entered Central Park. Sunday couples loitered. The sun blazed. Children skipped and ran. A little girl blew bubble gum. A black boy sat on a bench reading a comic magazine. A cloud of pigeons whirled in wild freedom in the sky and he could see their taut, almost transparent wings. He found an

empty bench and sat. He was hungry, but the idea
of food nauseated him. Nervously he rubbed his
damp palm across his eyes. Blast it all, *what* was
he to do?

He fell into a tense brooding, trying to reorder his
situation into a meaningful design. Yes; that foolish
Mrs. Blake was the cause of all his trouble . . . Had
she been the kind of mother she should have been,
none of this would have happened. His eyes nar-
rowed as recollection brought to his mind the kind
of images that proved his thesis.

He recalled that one Sunday morning he had gone
down in the elevator and Mrs. Blake had been waiting on the first floor; she'd been so tipsy that he'd
caught her arm to keep her from stumbling as she'd
entered the elevator. At the time he'd been disgusted and amused, but now his memory of that
incident made him seethe with moral rage. He should
have complained about her then, should have protested the right of a morally depraved woman like
her to live in the building.

Suddenly his condemnation of Mrs. Blake was
buttressed by still another and stronger memory.
About a year ago he'd been awakened around five
o'clock one morning by a strange noise—a dim, regu-
lar and rhythmic creaking—which had soon stopped.
He'd lain in bed puzzled, wondering what could have
been happening. A week later—it had been around
four o'clock in the morning this time—he'd heard
that same vague, rhythmic noise, and this time he'd
known with a dismaying flash of intuition what was
happening. . . . He'd gotten up and changed rooms,
converting his living room into his bedroom to escape
overhearing Mrs. Blake's carnal activities . . . Yes;
that was the kind of woman she was, and he was

more than ever certain that the true guilt for the
death of Tony lay not on his, but her shoulders.

He licked his lips and stared unseeingly through
the yellow sunshine. There was trying to break into
his mind yet another recollection, but he was fighting it off . . . Why? He bent forward and squinted
at the green grass and his mind drifted. He recalled
one evening last month when the summer sky was
still light and he'd come home early from the office
and had found little Tony alone upon the sidewalk.
The child had smiled and run skippingly toward
him, grabbing his hand.

"Hi, Mr. Fowler!" Tony had greeted him.

"Hello, Tony. How are you?" he'd asked him.

"Fine."

"What are you doing?"

"Playing."

"How's your mother?"

"Dunno. I ain't seen her today yet. She's sleeping."

"Oh."

"Are you tired, Mr. Fowler?"

"No, Tony. Why?"

"Are you very busy now?"

"Not at all. Why?"

"Talk to me some, hunh? A little," Tony had
begged.

He had looked into those round, large, black
eyes—helpless eyes, lonely eyes.

"Why, sure, Tony. But haven't you got anybody to
talk to?"

Tony's lips had quivered and he had not answered.

"Where are your little playmates? Don't you talk
to them?"

"Naw. I never talk to nobody. No friends around
here wanna play with me. . . ."

"Why?"

Again Tony had refused to answer; he'd looked off and frowned.

"All right, Tony. I'll talk to you. Let's go to the drugstore and get a malted milk, hunh? You don't think that your mother would mind, do you?"

"Naw. I won't tell her."

"But you should tell her everything you do," he told Tony. "Don't you?"

"Naw. Why should I?"

"Good boys do, you know."

"I'm bad..."

A stab of pity had gone through Erskine's heart as he'd stared at the child.

"Oh, no! Why do you say that?"

"Mama says so."

"Don't you tell your mother what you do during the day?"

"She never asks me what I do."

"But suppose you lose your appetite from drinking a malted milk," Erskine had posed a problem for him; "wouldn't your mother want to know why you won't eat?"

"Naw. She just fixes the supper and leaves it for me to eat when I wanna."

"But don't you talk to your mother at all?" he'd asked the child, leading him by the hand.

"She tells me to wash my face and not to make so much noise," Tony had said resentfully.

"Look, sometimes you must try telling her what you do during the day," Erskine had said. "Try it..."

"She won't listen—"

"But, Tony, your mother must talk to you sometimes—"

"But she won't tell me what she does," Tony had complained bitterly.

"Don't you love your mother?"

Tony had not answered.

"You should love your mother, you know, Tony."

"Maybe she doesn't want me to love her—"

"Why do you say that?"

"I dunno."

"Does she beat you often?"

"Naw. Sometimes... But I don't care."

"Then, what does she do to you to make you say that she doesn't want you to love her, Tony?"

"She never does anything. Mama's not like other ladies," Tony had said in confusion.

"Oh, Tony! You mustn't say that—"

"But that's what Mike who lives down the street says."

Erskine had been shocked. He'd patted Tony's head and had squeezed his hand in pity. There had been anger in his eyes as they'd entered the drug-store and seated themselves in a booth.

"Tony, you must not listen to what this Mike says—"

"But *all* the boys say that," Tony had informed him.

Erskine's understanding had been a remember-ing... If only he could help this abandoned child! Somebody ought to report that Mrs. Blake to the authorities... They were silent until their malted milks came and they sat sipping them through long straws.

"Why don't you ever come to see my mama?" Tony had asked him suddenly.

"She's never invited me," Erskine said, staring at the boy.

"Then why don't you call up and ask her to let you come over, like the others do?" Tony had de-manded hopefully.

"I guess I'm pretty busy, Tony," Erskine had answered uneasily.

"I like you better than I like the other men who come to see her," Tony had said, looking Erskine full in the face. "They won't talk to me. They take mama in the bedroom and lock the door."

"I like you, Tony. You're a good boy," Erskine had mumbled, avoiding Tony's eyes.

Offense nestled deep in Erskine's heart. Tony had so upset him that he wanted to leave. He hadn't known how to act or what to say. His pity for the child had made him remain.

"When you were a boy, did you sleep in bed with your mother?" Tony had asked in a far-away voice.

"I guess so. I really don't remember, Tony. Do you?"

"Yes; when there isn't a man in bed with her."

Erskine had wanted to tell Tony not to talk like that, but he felt that he hadn't the right to. He'd felt more intimidated with Tony at that moment than with any adult he could have named.

"Do you sleep with your mother often?" he'd found himself asking Tony.

"I used to. But there are so many men coming to see her at night now . . . I go to sleep in her bed when she's away at work at night, but when I wake up in the morning, I find that she's taken me out of her bed and put me in my bed, and there's a man in the bed with her," Tony had said, staring off into space.

"Tony, you must not talk like that!"

"But it's true," Tony had said.

"You *really* must love your mother, you know," Erskine had said in confusion.

"I do," Tony had said, quietly, sincerely. "But she loves so many other people."

Erskine had blinked. He clenched his fist until it showed white.

"Don't talk like that about your mother," Erskine begged.

Tony seemed not to hear; he was staring off intently, then he looked at Erskine and blinked.

"You know, you look a little like the man who slept with mama last night," Tony had said at last. "I saw mama kissing him."

Erskine had pushed his empty glass away. He felt soiled. Somebody ought to wring that Mrs. Blake's neck! She had no right to do that to a child! Tony emptied his glass and, in his effort to drink every drop, he made a loud noise by sucking air through the straws. His little face was grave, sober; he seemed to be staring at some image that baffled and frightened him.

"Mr. Fowler?" his voice had come with a soft hint of fear in it.

"Yes, Tony."

"Will *you* tell me something?"

"Sure. I'll tell you anything. But why do you ask me like that?"

"'Cause other people won't."

"What do you want to know, Tony?"

"Where do we all come from?"

"What do you mean?"

"How are people made?"

Erskine had smiled to reassure Tony.

"God makes us, Tony."

"*How?*"

"He creates us," Erskine had explained, wishing that Tony'd not ask any more questions.

Tony's eyes had fluttered distrustfully across Erskine's face.

"Don't you believe me, Tony?"

The child's eyes had filled with tears and he'd stared down into his empty glass.

"You're fooling me," he whimpered.

"No; I'm telling you the truth. Why don't you believe me?"

"Dunno."

Tony had mastered himself and was drying the tears.

"Tony, God made all people in the world—"

"Yes. But ..." Tony had stammered diplomatically.

"But what?"

"Mama didn't say that we are made like that."

"What did she say?"

"She said that men and women make babies—"

"Oh, sure; sure, Tony. They do. But God lets them make them—"

"Why?"

"For His glory. So little boys like you can have a chance to live," Erskine had explained, forcing a smile as he talked; but he knew that he'd not answered Tony and he wondered if it was his duty to do so.

"But *why?*" Tony had asked wailingly.

"Don't you think you ought to ask your mama about that, Tony? It's better for her to tell you—"

"But she won't tell me everything ... Now, you tell me why God makes the babies—"

"It's His will, God's will—"

"*Will?* What's will, Mr. Fowler?"

"Er—It's desire, Tony. When you desire something, you want it, you will it. Understand?"

"Then God wants them to be angry?" Tony had asked, frowning.

Erskine had blinked. What was the child getting at?

"Angry? Why, no, my boy. Why do you say 'angry'?"

"I mean the man and the woman—God wants 'em to be *angry?*"

"No. Tony, a husband loves his wife, and then there's a baby—"

"No!" Tony had exploded with sudden vehemence. "You're not telling me the truth—"

"But I *am* telling the truth, Tony!"

"But they *fight*... I've *seen* 'em fighting. *Then* there's a baby—"

"Fighting? What do you mean, Tony?" he had asked, but his words had slipped out of his mouth before he'd known it, and now he regretted his asking.

"One night I saw a big man fight mama," Tony had explained. "Mama didn't have any clothes on, and the man didn't have any clothes on either. And mama said that she was scared that she'd have a baby. Mr. Fowler—" Tony had paused and looked hard at Erskine, "why do they have to fight like that to make babies?"

Erskine's mind had reeled. What hadn't this five-year-old child seen? And yet Erskine had known that he had been reacting to more than what Tony had been telling him. Tony's words had made him remember, and his head had swum, and he'd wanted to rise and run from this... But a nameless weight anchored him to his seat.

"Tell me, why do they fight like that?" Tony had asked again, insistently, worriedly.

"I don't know, Tony," Erskine had said under his breath. "Little boys mustn't bother about such things..." What else could he say?

"Then my mama knows *more* than you do," Tony had declared in triumph.

Erskine had known that he had to be careful. He could not give this child an explanation that would make him repeat his words to his mother, for his mother might well come to him and bawl him out for it.

"Maybe she does," Erskine had sighed in defeat.

"But you are a man," Tony had argued. "You can find out. People will tell you anything—"

"I guess I don't want to ask them, Tony," he had said wearily.

Tony had stared off again, then his lips quivered.

"I don't want to grow up," he had said at last. "I don't wanna be a man—"

"Why?"

"'Cause I don't wanna fight," he said. "I don't wanna fight ladies like my mother..."

Erskine had not answered that. He had been determined to stop the conversation. Yes; he'd take Tony to the toy shop down the street and buy him something to distract him. That was as good a way as any of getting out of this horrible atmosphere of panic and degradation that Tony evoked around him.

"Say, Tony, wouldn't you like some toys from the store down the street?"

Tony's eyes had grown round.

"For real?"

"Sure."

"I wanna long-range bomber," Tony had said with excitement. "The kind that carries the atom bomb."

"All right. But do you think they've got them there?"

"Sure. I've seen 'em in the windows."

Erskine had paid and had sauntered out, thoughtfully leading Tony by the hand. The child chatted about a film he'd seen in which fighter planes had been in a big battle in the skies. Erskine had brooded pityingly over the child, a frown creasing his forehead. Tony had felt Erskine's silence and had stopped stiffly; he'd lifted his little face in fear toward Erskine.

"Are you angry with me, Mr. Fowler?" Tony had asked anxiously.

"God, no! No, Tony—"

"I thought maybe you were thinking of fighting me—"

"No; no . . . You mustn't *think* of such things!" Erskine said in a frenzy.

"But if somebody's going to fight you, you must always try to know it," Tony had said, reasoning and frowning.

"Why, Tony?"

"So you can run and save yourself," the child had told him.

"But I'm not going to fight you, Tony," Erskine had pleaded with Tony. "I'm your friend."

"For real?" Tony had asked with rising inflections of voice.

"For real, Tony," Erskine had said in the tone of one swearing an oath.

Erskine became aware of the strong, yellow sun, the green grass, the distant, tall apartment hotels looming across Central Park. Could it have been *that* that had frightened poor little Tony? Was it *possible?* He had the sensation that reality was dissolving before his eyes. Tony had been living in an unreal world, a dream, and, by accident, he had become a figment of Tony's dream, a frightening figment which had scared Tony into falling . . . Erskine sighed, his eyes glistening, staring without seeing. Now that he was thinking of poor Tony, he

recalled the rest of that strange summer evening
when the sun had stayed so long in the skies.

With Tony holding his hand, Erskine had walked
in silence toward the toy store. When they reached
the brightly colored, toy-arrayed windows, they
paused.

"Now, which plane do you want, Tony?" he had
asked the child.

Tony's eyes had danced with interest. Carefully,
he searched over every toy in the window before
answering. Then he pointed directly to the four-
engine bombing planes.

"That bomber *there*, with the little baby fighter
under the stomach," Tony had said breathlessly.
Then he'd whirled abruptly and stared pleadingly
into Erskine's face. "Could I have *two* of them,
please?"

"*Two?*" Erskine had asked. "But why two?"

"I wanna mama bomber and a papa bomber, and
the little baby bombers with 'em," Tony had explained.

"Oh, all right," Erskine had agreed uneasily; he
was detecting a morbid drift in the child's preoccupations and it disturbed him. But why not buy
him two of them if he wanted them? The least thing
he could do was to be kind to an emotionally de-
prived child, an emotionally violated child.

He had followed Tony into the store and had
stood beside him as he had selected a gray bomber
and a blue bomber, both with little "baby" fighter
planes tucked under their bellies. On the sidewalk
once more, Tony had confided boastfully to him:

"I like bombers."

"Really? Why?"

"I make 'em fight," Tony had said with a trace of
defiance and dread in his voice.

"That's good," Erskine had said with feigned cheerfulness.

What was happening to the child? His curiosity was leading him toward finding out, yet he was checked by a sense of shame. It wouldn't be right to lead the child to tell him too much. In the fading light of a red, setting sun that spilled over the tops of tall apartment buildings, Erskine had paused when Tony had stopped, squatted, and placed his two bombers on the sidewalk. Passers-by glanced and smiled at the tall man and the little boy and the bombing planes. Then, puffing out his cheeks and making a sound that imitated the drone of planes in flight, Tony, holding the gray bomber in his left hand and the blue bomber in his right, made them veer and loop at imaginary speeds by circling his arms high above his head and then sweeping them low toward the pavement.

"What are the planes doing, Tony?" he asked timidly, half afraid.

"They're looking for the enemy," Tony had said, continuing his game.

"Who's the enemy?"

"Anybody . . ."

The motors of Tony's planes had droned louder as he lifted them as high in the air as he could.

"They're climbing into the sky now!" Tony had panted. "They're going out over the ocean . . . ! Everybody's scared . . . ! *Look!* Here comes the enemy bombers! There's gonna be a *fight*, a big *fight* . . . ! Watch! The big bombers are letting the little baby bombers drop out of their stomachs! The sky's full of little baby fighter planes now . . . Everybody's *fighting* . . . !"

In spite of his shame, Erskine had watched little Tony's face grow white with fear as he pursued his make-believe game of "fighting," and Erskine felt ill.

"Look!" Tony was screaming now with a mixture of compulsive terror and fascination in his face. "The little baby fighters are falling down . . . !"

Sweat had stood on Tony's face and his body trembled. He looked wildly about, as though seeing something that Erskine could not see. Suddenly he dropped the planes; then, in an effort to find shelter from his self-created nightmare, he grabbed Erskine's legs, shut his eyes, and clung to him frantically.

"What's the matter, Tony?" Erskine had asked him, holding him.

"Oh! Oh! I'm so *scared,*" Tony had whimpered.

"Now, now," Erskine had said. "It's nothing. Don't cry! I'm here with you . . ."

In the end Erskine too had grown frightened, for he could feel what was frightening the child. What could he do for Tony? He's all mixed up . . . He ought to talk to Mrs. Blake about Tony . . . But had he the right to interfere? He had stooped and gathered up the bombing planes from the sidewalk and handed them to Tony. But Tony would not take them; he backed off, shaking his head, turning his face away.

"I don't want 'em; I don't want 'em," Tony had sobbed, flinging out his hands.

"But they're yours, Tony," he'd tried to persuade the child. "Take 'em and keep 'em."

"They *scare* me; they *scare* me!" he'd sobbed.

Tony had started running towards the entrance of the building. Erskine had been of a mind to run after him, to try to comfort him, but he checked himself. The bombing planes suddenly felt loathsome in his hands and he had an impulse to toss

them into the street. But, no . . . He'd be acting like
Tony if he did that . . . He sighed, picturing Tony
hiding and sobbing somewhere, trembling and brooding over images of life much too big and complicated for him. He took the abandoned bombing
planes and gave them to Mrs. Westerman.

"Just keep these for Tony, won't you?" he'd asked
her. "He forgot them and left them on the sidewalk."

"He, he—" Mrs. Westerman had chuckled. "That
child's a case. He's always doing that. He's a queer
child, he is . . . He plays alone, then gets scared and
runs off and leaves his toys."

"Does he do that all the time?"

"*All* the time," Mrs. Westerman had said, shaking
her head. "He's scared of something . . ."

Erskine had been so angry and depressed that he
had not wanted to eat his dinner that night.

He still sat hunched on the bench in Central Park,
staring at the green grass long after the images of
Tony's tortured fare and his bombing planes had
vanished from his mind. Good God . . . *Now,* he
understood it. Yes, poor little Tony had thought that
he, naked, frantic, wild-eyed, had been about to
fight him and fear had made him lose his balance
and topple . . . Christ, were there happenings like
that in this world? Were there shadows of that
density lurking behind these bright, straight streets?
He longed to discuss this with somebody, but he
felt that at the very moment of uttering his words
to describe it, its reality would somehow vanish.
Strangely, the accident had happened more than
four hours ago, and it was not until this moment
that he had realized the truth.

Brooding, the memory of his own long dead mother returned to him. Yes; he understood Tony. He

too recalled watching strange men tramping in and
out of the house in his childhood, and he felt a
surging sense of terror, old, buried, trying to re-
capture him. He cut the distasteful recollection short
by doubling his fists, rising and glaring about, ob-
livious of his surroundings. He muttered out loud:
"Women oughtn't to do things like that..."

Again his emotions became religious. The cer-
tainty he had felt in church returned. He must somehow redeem what had happened to Tony! *That was
it!* Conviction hardened in him. In redeeming Tony,
he'd be redeeming himself. How neatly the double
motives fitted! He'd help to purge the world of such
darkness... How right he'd been in refusing to accept blame for Tony's death; it hadn't been his fault
at all. Only an ignorantly lustful woman could spin
such spider webs of evil to snare men and innocent
children! As he walked he told himself with the
staunchest conviction of his life: "That Mrs. Blake's
the guilty one..."

He entered a cafeteria and toyed absently with a
plate of food. On the sidewalk again, he headed
slowly toward home. In the lower hallway of the
building he met Mrs. Westerman.

"What about Tony?" he asked her.

Mrs. Westerman shook her head and closed her
eyes.

"Ah, that poor thing... God bless his soul... He
died still holding that toy pistol of his," she said. "I
think it was one you gave him."

"Did they find out how he fell?"

"He was just playing and fell," Mrs. Westerman
told him. "That's what the Medical Examiner said.
And, of course, the child never regained consciousness."

"Is there anything I can do for Mrs. Blake?" he asked her.

Mrs. Westerman let her deep, gray eyes rest meltingly on Erskine's face.

"You're so kind, Mr. Fowler," she sighed. "Tony was so fond of you. He spoke of you all the time. Told me many times that he wished you were his daddy ... He was so alone, that child." Mrs. Westerman shook her head and closed her eyes again. "Lord, I don't know ..." Her voice trailed off.

"What do you mean, Mrs. Westerman?" Erskine asked, sensing that she was about to say something about Mrs. Blake.

"I just don't know," Mrs. Westerman repeated significantly.

"What are you talking about?" Erskine demanded, hugging his Bible and Sunday-school-book tightly, feeling tension entering him.

"I'm not one to judge others, Mr. Fowler," Mrs. Westerman said, looking Erskine full in the face.

"You can speak frankly to me," he told her.

Mrs. Westerman drew a deep breath, waved her hand in front of her eyes as though to brush aside a repellant image, and then lifted her hands in a gesture of disgust.

"*That* woman ... And she calls herself a mother," Mrs. Westerman sighed again. Plainly she wanted to be coaxed to talk.

"Yes," Erskine said, feeling relieved, "I understand."

"She's upstairs now. Just got back from the undertaker, she did. She's just shattered. But she blames everybody but herself for what happened. She says she wants to sue the building for letting that railing be loose like that ... Says she's sure somebody must've been on that balcony—"

"What?" Erskine asked in suppressed alarm. "Somebody on the balcony. Somebody with Tony?"

"She's hinting at something like that—"

"But what does she mean?" he asked, striving to appear calmer.

"God only knows..."

"Does she think that somebody pushed Tony off?"

"She didn't say... You can hardly talk to her. She was weeping and vomiting... She says that she thinks she saw a naked person on the balcony..."

Erskine was petrified. Terror rose so hotly in his chest that for a moment he could not breathe. He struggled for speech.

"*What?*" He remembered that he had to control himself. "That's *my* balcony... What's she talking about? A naked *man?*" Mrs. Westerman had not used the word "man," and Erskine knew that he ought not to have used it. "What is this, Mrs. Westerman?"

Mrs. Westerman caught hold of Erskine's arm and whispered: "Come in here a moment, Mr. Fowler. I want to talk to you in private..."

He followed her inside her dingy apartment; he stood stiffly, looking around at the shabby, over-stuffed furniture. She had caught him completely off balance and he regretted having allowed himself to evince so much surprise. He'd change his attitude at once.

"What is this you're trying to tell me, Mrs. Westerman?" he asked her rather roughly, reverting to his businessman's attitude. But he was really asking himself if he shouldn't have told the police after all.

"Listen," Mrs. Westerman whispered to him, obviously relishing her role. "She had a man in her apartment until five this morning, see? That's the kind of woman she is..."

"Oh! But I thought she said that she was sleeping when Tony fell—"

"She was; she claims—"

"Then how could she see somebody on my balcony?"

"She says she got up once to signal to Tony not to make so much noise," Mrs. Westerman explained. "Then she says that she went back to bed ... For a long while, she says, she didn't hear anything ... She got worried, thinking that Tony had gone down into the street ... She then went to her window again and couldn't see Tony. Now, here's the funny part of it ... She says that she saw feet ... somebody's *feet* dangling in the air ... She says that she thought that it was some other child playing with Tony, you understand? I'll tell you her very words ... 'Naked feet dangling in the air' ... Can you imagine that? Maybe she was drunk; she admits she'd been drinking a little ... Mr. Fowler, I could still smell liquor on her breath when she went down with me in the elevator to see Tony's little body lying there ..." Mrs. Westerman shrugged. "Or maybe she's all mixed up, in a kind of fog or something; you know? Maybe she's remembering the man who was with her, hunh? Could be, couldn't it, Mr. Fowler? She feels guilty now and she's trying to think up something out of thin air to take the blame off of her ..."

"But I don't understand," Erskine protested, blinking. "Why, that's my balcony ... I heard nobody out there but Tony; he was beating his drum ... And how could she talk of seeing someone *naked* out *there* ... ?" He choked, but managed to continue. "And what's all that got to do with Tony's falling?"

"Nothing, if you ask me, Mr. Fowler," Mrs. Westerman said stoutly. "And my husband'll say the same thing. He's not here now; he's down at the police station trying to answer all their damn-fool questions. Listen, I think she was drunk, drunk as a coot. I think she was confused and I'd say so in court under oath, so help me God."

"But how could she see onto my balcony?" Erskine asked. He knew well that she could see his balcony, but he thought it best to establish his ignorance of that; he wanted to be totally innocent of everything connected with Tony's falling.

"From her kitchen window, if she leaned out a little—"

"Oh," he breathed, pretending surprise, "I didn't know that."

"She can get a tiny glimpse of your balcony... But, Mr. Fowler, she didn't see anything; take my word for it," Mrs. Westerman swore. "I told her to her face that I doubted if she saw anything or anybody on the balcony but Tony... Listen, Mr. Fowler, she's just like all these loose women; they're a dime a dozen... When somebody catches 'em with a man, they start yelling: 'Rape!' it's a wonder she didn't say it was a nigger she saw. You understand?"

"I understand," Erskine said, nodding.

" 'Naked feet dangling in the air' on the balcony," Mrs. Westerman repeated Mrs. Blake's words in a tone of derision. "And, would you believe it, she said that those feet were going up, mind you; those naked feet were going up in the air! When I told her that that was impossible, she switched back to that damned iron railing..."

"Say, just how drunk was she when she went down this morning to see Tony?" Erskine asked her shrewdly.

"Ha!" Mrs. Westerman exclaimed dramatically, rolling her eyes at him. She sucked her lungs full of air and launched out: "Listen, Mr. Fowler, you haven't heard *anything* yet ... When that woman started talking to me about 'naked feet dangling in the air,' 'naked feet going up,' I asked her real sweet-like: 'What feet are you talking about, Mrs. Blake? Tell me, what color were these feet?' Well, she started blinking and stalling and then she said: 'White, of course, all feet are white ...' 'Are *all* feet white, Mrs. Blake?' I asked her. 'Maybe they were colored feet,' I suggested to her. She fell for it, hook, line and sinker, and she says to me: 'No; it wasn't a colored person's feet ...' She didn't catch on; then I says to her, I did: 'Listen here, Mrs. Blake, maybe they were *pink* feet you saw?' And then, still innocent as a child, she says to me, shaking her head: 'What do you mean? I'm not blind! I know what I saw!' Then I says to her: 'I ain't saying you're blind, but I want you to describe those feet to me ... Now, just how *many* feet did you see, Mrs. Blake?' She thinks a minute, then says: 'Two. I saw *two* feet.' 'Going up in the air?' I asks. 'Yes; going up,' she says. I showed her my foot (I was wearing my house slippers then) and I says to her: 'My feet are pink, see? Now, were the feet you saw, were they *pink*, like mine?'

She thinks a minute, then she says, real quick-like: 'Yes; I guess they were pink.' Ha, ha ... Mr. Fowler, I had her *right* where I wanted her. Now, Mr. Fowler, I'm no drinker myself, but I know a lush when I see one. So I says to her: 'Mrs. Blake, tell me, just how *many* toes did each foot have?' She blinked again, like she didn't know what I was getting at. Really, when you get right down to it, she's kinda stupid, you know. She started mumbling about how everybody mistreats her and so forth, then she wanted to know: 'What are you talking about? 'Feet have *five* toes. Everybody knows that. Why, you're

talking like you think I didn't see feet...' 'Hunh,
hunh,' I says to her. 'Now, look here, Mrs. Blake,
feet have five toes, but was *one* toe very long? One
toe was *very* long, wasn't it?' 'What do you mean?'
she asks me. 'One toe being very *long?*' 'Look,' I
says, 'we all have a big toe, don't we? Now, was
one toe very, *very* long?'' She still didn't get the point;
I had to spell it out to her. 'Listen here, Mrs. Blake,'
I says. 'If the *big* toes on those *pink* feet you saw
were very long—long like snouts, like *elephant* trunks,
then I understand it all? See? You saw pink elephants, dearie! Not feet! Maybe you had a mild
case of D.T.'s, hunh? You saw little pink elephants
going up, floating in the air... Now, get some sense
in your head and stop all this crazy talk about seeing
naked feet... If you don't, I'll tell those cops just
how drunk you really were, you hear?' Well, Mr.
Fowler, that shut her up good and clean. She
clamped her mouth and she hasn't breathed another word about 'naked feet dangling in the air,'"
Mrs. Westerman finished on a note of high triumph.
"Mr. Fowler, that woman won't talk about naked
feet again, I assure you."

Erskine was numb. He had to see that woman;
he had to do something and soon...

"Are you sure she's in now?" he asked her.

"Oh, sure; she's up here. And do you know, with
all of her goings and comings, she's as much as admitted to me that she hasn't got a single, real,
honest-to-goodness friend she can turn to now? *Nobody!* Can you beat that? May God strike me dead,
but many's the time she's rolled up here at that
door—" Mrs. Westerman pointed dramatically "—in
a big shiny car at two or three o'clock in the morning, half drunk, swaying like a sheet on a clothes-
line as she walked... And always some cheap little

punk waving at her from the car before he drove off... Of course, sometimes they went up with her, but don't ask me what they did! Now, she's *alone*... What kind of *friends* did she have, I ask you?"

"God only knows," Erkine sighed.

"Yes, God only knows," Mrs. Westerman readily relished the phrase and rolled it on her tongue. She shook her head. "It's a pity that a fine, Christian man like you has to be bothered with the likes of her, Mr. Fowler. Oh, that Mrs. Blake... She sure upset us all today. My poor husband came tearing in here, white as flour, asking me to phone upstairs and tell Mrs. Blake that her son was hurt. Would you believe it? I had to wait on that phone till she was sober enough to understand what I was saying ... That phone rang *six* times before it could wake her out of a drunken sleep..."

"Tsk, tsk, tsk," Erskine clucked his tongue and shook his head; his legs were trembling.

"Well, let's all hope for the best," Mrs. Westerman sang, throwing a bright, ironic smile at Erskine.

"Yes. Well, see you later," Erskine said.

He rode up in the elevator, thinking: *She saw someone on the balcony... But she isn't sure...* Good God! She was close... Would she tell the police what she had seen, or had Mrs. Westerman's scornful rejection of her confused perceptions made her hesitate? He entered his apartment and stared at the bulk of the unread Sunday paper. How like a dream it all was! No; it was real. Tony's death was real; Tony's timid questions about where babies came from were real... He lay on his unmade bed and the afternoon wore on. The sky grew gradually dark and deep shadows entered the room. He rose and stared moodily out of his open window at the window of Mrs. Blake's living room and was sur-

prised to see a light burning there. Her window was
up too. Go and see her now . . . No; wait . . . Wait
for what? He didn't know.

He gave a start as his phone rang. He picked up
the receiver and heard a dim hum, and back of that
hum he caught the faint sounds of street traffic,
honking of auto horns, a policeman's whistle . . .

"Hello," he called into the phone.

Silence.

"Hello, hello," he repeated.

Still silence, but the sounds of street traffic were
still audible.

"Hello!" he raised his voice, his eyes worried.

The line clicked. Hmnnn . . . Had someone waited
just long enough to hear his voice, and then hung
up? He cradled the phone and stared. Had someone,
besides Mrs. Blake, seen him naked on that balcony?
But, if they had, wouldn't they have spoken to the
police about it before now? Oh, maybe *that* had
been Mrs. Blake? He rushed to his open window
and heard the sound of her television set: music
was playing. The sound he'd heard on the phone
was that of street traffic . . . He shook his head; he
was too wrought up; he was imagining things. Whoever had called would call again no doubt . . .

He sat on the edge of the bed and ran his fingers
though his damp hair. It was almost night. Restless,
he rose and stood at his window and stared at the
lights of the city. He spun round as his phone rang
again. He snatched it up and spoke:

"Hello!"

There was no answer. This time there was a ca-
cophony of faint voices, as though the transmitter on
the other end was picking up sounds in a bar or
restaurant. He darted to his open window and
peered into Mrs. Blake's living room. The clear

strains of music were still coming over ... Definitely, it was not Mrs. Blake who was phoning him.

"Hello, hello," he spoke frantically into the phone.

"Mr. Fowler ... ?" It was a distant, strained voice of a woman.

"Yes; this is Mr. Fowler speaking. What is it?"

No answer ...

"Yes? Who's speaking?"

"I saw what happened," a thin, tinny voice wailed in his ear.

The line clicked. Erskine felt that some giant hand had snatched him from contact with the living world and had lifted him high up into a cold region where there was no air to breathe. He jiggled the hook.

"Hello, hello," he whispered into the phone.

The line was dead.

There was now no doubt about it; he'd been seen by somebody other than Mrs. Blake ... But what was the motive? Blackmail? God, he ought to go to the police this moment, right now; he was a fool to blunder around like this in a stupid funk. It'd be said that his staying away from the police was proof of guilt. And the longer he waited, the more difficult it would be for him to justify his not having told the police right off. Indeed, if he went now, they'd certainly want to know why he'd waited so long ... And that was why he didn't go ... Cause was becoming effect, and effect cause.

He cradled the phone and a look of defiance came into his face. All right, suppose someone *had* seen him? So what? What had he done wrong? Nothing ... He'd wait and see what that woman who'd called him would do. He'd wait ... Why, he was acting as if he'd really killed Tony. If anyone had killed Tony, it was that confounded Mrs. Blake ...

He was alert, hearing sounds coming from his balcony, just outside of his bathroom window. Were the police examining that iron railing? No; not at this time of night...Maybe it was the superintendent? He'd go and see. And what was that balcony door doing open at this time of night, anyway? It was usually locked...Well, it was his balcony, wasn't it? He'd look. He went into the brightly lighted hallway and quickly opened the door to the balcony and a shaft of light from the hall ceiling fell upon the somber face of Mrs. Blake who had turned and was staring at him with parted lips and a look of fright in her large, dark eyes.

"Oh, Lord," she sighed, "you scared me."

"I'm sorry," he mumbled. "I heard someone here ...It's you, Mrs. Blake..."

She turned from him and hung her head. Did she suspect him of anything?

"I feel simply dreadful about Tony," he told her.

She wept softly with her head turned away, her body making a sharp silhouette against the blue-black density of the night sky. He saw that she'd been trying to drag the heavy electric hobbyhorse into the hallway. The superintendent had, no doubt, given her the key to the balcony door...She was dressed in a rose-colored nylon robe and a slight, rain-scented wind was making her tumbling black locks tremble about her face and eyes. His nostrils caught a whiff of an intriguing perfume. Erskine was seized by a state of numbed anxiousness.

"Oh, let me help you with that," he said, going to her.

"Don't bother," she muttered.

What did that sullen tone of voice mean?

"I'll help you." He spoke with an undertone of resentment.

She stared at him for a moment, then began weeping afresh, covering her face with her hands, leaning against the sagging iron railing which wobbled perilously as her weight impinged upon it.

"Be *careful!*" he told her, taking her arm and pulling her roughly from the edge of the balcony. "It's dangerous there..."

"I don't care," she whimpered.

"You don't know what you're saying," he told her.

"Poor Tony," she sobbed. "I feel like dying..."

"You must take care of yourself," he said.

She continued weeping as though she had not heard; she leaned now against the brick wall of the building. The thought shot through Erskine's mind that if she'd fallen accidentally over that iron railing, there'd be one person less to say that they'd seen him or "naked feet" on the balcony this morning... The idea created such instant horror in his mind—it was as though the idea had been pushed upon his attention by some force—that he was seized with pity for her and he sought at once for something to banish the notion, to cover it up. Touching the tips of the pencils in his inner coat pocket, he stared at her shuddering body and his fear and moral condemnation of her fled and he yearned to soothe her. Timidly, he patted her shoulder.

"There, now... You must brace up... I'll take these things inside for you. Where do you want them? In your apartment?"

"Yes," she gulped. Then she whispered: "Tony was so deeply fond of you." She coughed. "Next to me, he loved you most in this world..."

"And I loved him too," he said quickly.

As she leaned against the wall, she sobbed. He picked up the tricycle, a baseball bat, a toy rifle, and a drum and placed them in the hallway in front of her door. Was that image of those "naked feet dangling" in her mind still? He lifted the heavy electric hobbyhorse and put it in front of her apartment door; when he returned to the balcony, she'd gathered up the remaining toys. Gently he took the things from her and, with his left arm full, he guided her with his right down the hallway. She unlocked the door of her apartment and went in and stood, dabbing at her eyes and trying to control her twisting lips.

"Where do you keep this?" he asked.

"Just leave 'em," she managed to say.

"I'll put 'em away for you—"

"There, in the hall closet," she whimpered.

He stored away all the toys except the electric hobbyhorse which was too big for the closet.

"Where do you keep this?" he asked.

"I'll have to take it apart," she mumbled, sinking into a chair and weeping again, her bosom heaving.

Her wet cheeks and her trembling body chastened him; her grief was so genuine, so simple, that his conception of her as an evil, giant, entangling spider-mother seemed remote. She was a poor woman who needed counselling and understanding and her stricken humanity appealed to him powerfully. He did not take his eyes off her until she looked at him.

He saw that the hobbyhorse was attached by bolts to a metal base containing an electric motor.

"Have you a screwdriver?" he asked her.

"No. But there's a knife in the kitchen. It's what I use," she gasped, trying to stem her weeping. But the tears continued to stream down her face.

He flicked on the light in the kitchen and searched in a table drawer and found a big, sharp, butcher knife. Five minutes later he had the hobbyhorse

taken apart and stored away in the closet. Holding
the knife, he stood over her. She still wept, her face
hidden in her arms.

"Is there something else you want me to do?" he
asked her, his eyes searching over her slumped form.

She straightened and, seeing the knife, leaped
from her chair and backed off with terror in her
face.

"What's the matter?" he asked, feeling terror too.

"That *knife* ... Don't point it at me like that ... I
can't stand knives!" she cried.

He looked down in surprise at the knife in his
hand; he had forgotten that he was holding it.

"I'm sorry," he mumbled.

Was she afraid of him? Did she think that he'd
killed Tony and was now trying to kill her? He put
the knife in the kitchen; when he returned, she
forced a smile.

"I'm sorry ... I act so silly," she apologized.

"You are a little unstrung," he commented.

They were silent. He recalled that awful thought
that he'd had about her falling off the balcony, as
Tony had fallen, and now he was wondering what
she'd seen in his face to make her leap up in terror
when he'd stood over her with that knife in his hand
... He had to struggle to overcome thoughts of
death about her and it made him almost hysterically
anxious to help her. It was only when he was reacting to her distress that he felt right about her.

"You've been so kind," she murmured. "God, I
must look a sight ..." She cocked her head and her
right hand fussed nervously with her disordered hair.

"I wish I could be of some help to you," he
mumbled humbly. "After all, Tony was a little friend
of mine. I used to talk with him a lot, you know ..."

Her eyes rested full on him with that same blank,

bleak stare that he'd seen that morning; or was he
imagining it ... ?

"He babbled about you always," she said, closing
her eyes. "He hadn't had much of a father in his
little life, and he was always talking of your being
his father ..." She flashed a twisted, shy smile that
begged forgiveness. "Just a child's notion," she explained, turning her head away quickly to hide her
trembling lips.

"He was a lonely child, wasn't he?" he ventured
to ask, remembering Tony's fear that early skylit
evening when he'd been frightened by his "fighting"
bombing planes.

She stared and lowered her head guiltily, like a
scolded child.

"I'm afraid he was," she said, sighing. "Next year
he would have been in the country. Now, he's gone
... I can't believe it."

She looked at him, then her eyes fell; a wistful
smile flitted across her lips as she murmured: "He
was always asking for a father ..." She stood abruptly, turned, her eyes blinded with tears. Her
hand groped for the jamb of the door and she
stumbled. He seized her arm and guided her to a
sofa in her living room and helped her down on it.
A floor lamp with a deep tan shade shed a bright
cone of yellow light upon her cascading black hair,
the creamy, satiny skin of her naked arms, the
throbbing aliveness of her throat, the ripe fullness
of her breasts, and the helpless wetness of her face;
her right leg, tapering and slanting, almost lost in
shadow, extended at an angle across the rug and
terminated in a tiny foot jammed tightly into a black
pump shoe and it made a lump rise in his throat ...
Suddenly she slid down upon the sofa until her
nylon, rose-colored robe fell away and her right

leg, nude to her thigh, sprawled with a dimpled knee. With shut eyes she keened a low, tense moan: "Tony . . . Tony . . . Tony . . ."

She twisted her body round and buried her face in the back of the sofa, as though yearning to escape the presence of an implacably monstrous world. Erskine felt pinioned in space. A fleeting glimmer of intuition made him suspect her of playing the role of an emotional *agent provocateur* to lure him into disclosing what he knew, but the notion was too far-fetched and he dismissed it from his mind. Blending in one wild wave, shame, anger, and guilt rose in him. His feelings were trying fumblingly to resolve themselves into something definite about the woman; but she hovered before him elusive, now threatening, now appealing . . . As she continued to weep, a part of her left breast showed and he could see a dark reddish tint circling the nipple, glowing like a shy shadow through her nylon brassiere. He was transfixed, swamped by a hot desire to protest her nudity, yet he could not take his eyes off her. And her nudity was so clearly, unintentionally the product of a pounding grief shattering her that all her blatant sensuality seemed redeemed, annihilated. So ransomed was her sexuality by her suffering that he wanted to get to his knees and beg her to forgive him, to absolve him for having accidentally scared poor Tony to death . . .

As he watched her lithe body writhe on the sofa, he recalled Mrs. Westerman's having said that she had seen "naked feet dangling" on his balcony . . . Fear slowed the beat of his heart. Was she acting? How did one take a woman like this? He strove to simplify his emotions about her, and he couldn't. He wanted to reach out and cover her nakedness, hide it from his eyes, but he stood and studied her irresistible plush curves, tracing the gentle slope of her thighs, gaping as though hypnotized.

Her words rang again in his mind: *He was always talking of your being his father* ... His feelings played with the notion; he struggled against it, but found himself wondering how it would have been if he'd tried being Tony's father ... It would've meant being married to a *fallen* woman like this! Inwardly he flinched, feeling his feelings realizing the idea of being with her. *Damn this woman!* Her mere presence exuded evil; that was why notions like this were in his mind ... And a man had had her until five o'clock this morning! That ancient jealousy that he'd thought he'd thrust back of him forever rose now from the forgotten, dusty graveyard of his emotions and lived in him again; he was being claimed by that which he thought he'd surmounted long ago with God's help and his incessant toil ... That uneasiness in the presence of a woman, that deep conviction that no woman could ever be truly his; that, even if he were even so lucky as to marry her, something untoward would happen to snatch her away from him—that was the torment that was churning in him now.

But how in God's name could such thoughts enter his head? He was the superintendent of the Mount Ararat Baptist Sunday School; he could not entertain the idea of marrying a degraded woman like this. To whom could he ever introduce her? Why, then, had the notion of being married to her popped into his head? Yes; he'd been seeking a way to silence her if she made trouble for him by repeating her story of seeing "naked feet dangling" on the balcony ... He'd have to find some other solution ...

Yet, she was so broken, abandoned ... But was this not his chance to save this woman, to own her, to hold her in his arms so that no one *could, would want* to claim her? The idea moved him as much toward revulsion as toward compassion, as much toward wanting to slap her as toward wanting to caress her—to fling her from his sight or take her and tell her what life could mean, *ought* to mean ... He mopped clumsily at the sweat on his face. In him something was teetering, reeling as Tony had when he had lost his footing and tumbled from the balcony ...

"You know, you must take hold of yourself." He made himself speak, amazed at how compassionate his tone was.

She grew still and glared stonily before her.

"Nobody knows anything of my life." She spoke in a bitter tone.

"That's right," he urged her softly, "go ahead and talk. It'll help you ..."

"They're saying all kinds of things about me—"

"Who?"

"That awful Mrs. Westerman, and the others too," she said. She stared at him sulkily and mumbled. "And maybe you too, for all I know—"

"Oh, no!" he protested, blushing. She was like a mistreated child now and he felt more confident as his mind encompassed the narrow range of her reactions. The simpler she was, the safer he felt. "Now, now ... You mustn't let things like that bother you," he told her soothingly, remembering that, just a few hours ago, he'd agreed heartily with Mrs. Westerman.

"That Mrs. Westerman's saying it's all *my* fault," she whimpered. "And God knows what else she's saying about me ... But how could I help what happened? I work nights ..."

He wanted to ask her if she'd been drunk, as Mrs. Westerman had said, but he decided not to.

"You work?" he asked gently, leading her to talk.

"Of course I do," she said, showing astonishment that he should ask. "How do you think I live? I'm not rich—"

"What kind of work do you do?" he asked.

"I have the hat-check concession in the *Red Moon*." She spoke with a certain defiance.

"The *Red Moon*? What's that?"

"A nightclub," she said flatly. "And it's hard to make ends meet, really. I've got five other girls employed with me on a percentage basis. After rent, expenses, and the kickback I have to give to the nightclub owner, what have I left? Just enough to get by on ... I wanted so much to hire a colored woman to look after Tony, but I'd have to pay fifty dollars a week. I can't afford it. And I work such long, long hours ... That's why I always come home so late. And God knows what people think I'm doing ... How could I look after Tony and earn my living at the same time?" Her voice died in her throat.

More sinned against than sinning, he told himself with satisfaction, relishing the advantage that his money and social status gave him over her.

"I've never been in a nightclub," he told her musingly.

"Really?" She stared at him. "Well, working in a nightclub's just like working any other place ... The people who have fun in such places are not those who work in them."

"I guess you're right," he said.

"There's no guessing about it." She spoke bitterly. "Try it once."

"Do you have to drink and dance with the customers?" he asked.

She hesitated, then said: "I wear a little costume; it's to go with the atmosphere of the place."

"Oh, I see . . ." He tried to picture how she would look. "But, listen here, you mustn't let gossip bother you—"

"But it *does!*" she protested, doubling her fists. "What can *one* person be responsible for in this world? I depend on nobody. The least I ask for is that I be let *alone!*"

She pulled up and saw her leg was exposed; she closed her robe and reddened. It was as he would have had it; she had unwittingly bared herself and now he liked that tardy gesture of modesty.

"Forgive me," she murmured, "I'm almost out of my mind."

Just how tenaciously was she contending that she'd seen "naked feet dangling"? Now was the time to test her . . .

"Tell me," he began innocently, "how *did* Tony happen to fall like that?"

"God, I don't know . . ." Her eyes went blank and she shook her head.

"Were you asleep?"

"I guess so," she drawled vaguely.

"Look here," Erskine said, getting to the point, "this Mrs. Westerman's telling people that you saw somebody *push* Tony off the balcony—"

"Oh, God, no!" She leaped to her feet and her eyes blazed. "I didn't say *that!* That *woman!*"

Erskine felt that her response was too defensive for her to be certain of herself.

"Did you see someone?" he asked her.

She took a deep breath, stared at Erskine guiltily, bit her lips, and sighed. Erskine could see that she was still smarting under Mrs. Westerman's intimidations.

"I thought I saw..." She broke off, abashed. "You see, there've been complaints about Tony's making so much noise. I was sleeping..." She paused, swallowed. "I got up when I heard Tony banging his drum. I waved at him—You know, I can see a tip of your balcony by leaning out of my kitchen window—Well, he saw me and he quieted down. That was the first time I looked...I went back to bed. Later a noise, like a pistol shot, woke me up. I thought that something'd happened to Tony. I ran to the kitchen window and looked out...I didn't see Tony. I thought maybe he'd gone downstairs, though I'd told him not to...After a while I still didn't hear 'im and I got worried...I ran into the hallway and peeped at 'im; he was playing like a little lamb, riding his hobbyhorse. I went back to sleep..."

As she talked Erskine felt that he was walking barefooted over red hot coals. She'd heard his door when it had slammed shut! And she'd been out into the hallway while he'd been weirdly riding up and down, naked and sweating, in the elevator! Good God! It's a wonder that he'd not bumped into her!

"...but Tony was so quiet that I got worried. You know how it is with children; when they make noise, you want 'em to stop; but when they're quiet, *too* quiet, you get to thinking that maybe something's gone wrong...When I tried to see him this time—leaning out of my kitchen window—I couldn't. I called and he didn't answer. Then I was sure he'd disobeyed me and had gone down into the street. I was about to turn away from the window when I saw...I thought I saw—I know it sounds crazy—but I thought I saw naked feet dangling in the air, going up..."

"Naked feet?" Erskine tried to make his voice sound disbelieving; he felt sweat on his face.

"That's what I *thought* I saw," she mumbled, blinking, begging him with her eyes to believe her.

"But what do you *mean?*" he demanded.

"It sounds odd, I know," she agreed. "The super and his wife, that Mrs. Westerman, won't believe me. They don't like me, anyway . . . But that's what I saw . . ."

"You *think* you saw that?" he asked her pointedly.

"I saw feet . . . real f-feet; they w-were going u-up—" She broke off in confusion and her face reddened.

"You think that somebody was on that balcony with Tony?"

"I don't know. But—"

"Maybe Tony fell from some *other* floor," he suggested. "He *did* play on other floors, didn't he?"

"Yes," she breathed, her eyes cast down. "That's true . . . Oh, God, I don't know!" She looked at him hopefully. "Maybe that was a workman I saw . . . ?"

"On a *Sunday* morning?" There was a trace of scorn in his voice. "And what would he be doing barefooted?"

"I don't know," she answered in a singsong voice.

"Maybe Tony pulled off his shoes and was climbing," he suggested. "Boys do things like that, you know, in the summertime—"

"No; no . . . These were *big* feet I saw," she asserted stoutly.

"Could you be certain of how big they were from that distance?" he asked in a district attorney's tone. "Maybe you were looking at *another* balcony—"

"I don't know; I don't know . . ."

"Are you sure that you didn't see a reflection or

something?" He pressed her gently, sympathetically.

"I know it sounds wild...You didn't hear anything on the balcony, did you?" she asked suddenly.

"Tony woke me up with his drum," he said easily. "Then I went back to sleep—"

"I'm sorry," she apologized; yet it was evident that she was not at all satisfied.

"Were you alone?" he questioned her, wanting to see if she'd lie about the man who had spent the night with her.

Resentment flickered in her eyes and two red spots bloomed in her cheeks and spread till her entire face burned. Yes; she knows that Mrs. Westerman has talked to me...

"Yes," she said uneasily, "at *that* time I was." She looked off, biting her lips.

She had evaded telling him the truth. A *little whore*...He felt more and more justified in not telling her that it was *his* feet dangling in the air that she had seen just before he had fallen through his window into the bathroom. Yet, clashing with his feeling of justification was a sense of anger and jealousy for her living so loosely, sloppily, for her giving herself so easily. He felt that she had no moral claim upon him, yet he wanted to save her, rescue her, and find out something about the strange man who'd spent the night with her...And, under it all, his heart was sullen and guilty because he realized that his emotions were hopelessly contradictory.

"If you'd seen 'naked feet' like that," he advised her with sudden coldness, "you should have called someone—"

"*Everybody's* telling me what I should have done!" she lamented, bursting into a wild sob. "I didn't *know*...Maybe I only *thought* I saw something

..." She was almost ready to give up her story. In despair she flung back her head and covered her eyes with her hands; her knees spread and the folds of her robe fell away and he was looking at the quick thickening of her thighs as they curved upward. Now, since his fear was abating, she was beginning to excite him all the more. She sat up at last and stared at him with full eyes clouded with tears and he could not meet her gaze.

"For Tony's sake, I'd like to help you in this," he told her haltingly.

"You're very kind . . ." She smiled at him suddenly, smiled with tears in her eyes. "It helps a lot when you can talk to somebody. I don't know why you bother with me. You know, I've always been a little scared of you."

"Why?"

"Well, I don't know really. You always seem so friendly, yet so faraway, in another world—"

"I'm not faraway at all, my dear," he told her, his confidence waxing, feeling that he had no need to be uneasy with her now.

"I'm no intellectual," she said, concerned with the impression that she was making. "I'm just a straight-from-the-shoulder, down-to-earth woman who says what she thinks. If I don't do or say the right thing, it's just because I don't always know what the right thing to say or do is . . ." She smiled a smile that indicated that, though she was humble, she knew her intrinsic worth.

"Don't let that bother you," he coaxed her.

Her face showed sudden consternation. She stood abruptly and placed the index finger of her right hand to her temple and shook her head.

"Lord, I've forgotten to get little Tony's clothes together," she wailed. "The undertaker wanted them as soon as possible ... I'm so worried that I don't know if I'm going or coming ..."

"Is there anything I can do?"

"I'm going to lay his little things out," she said, going into the next room.

Erskine sat and brooded. He'd help her; it was his duty to ... But what a woman! She had no more morals than a cat ... At last he now understood how she was able to live in the Elmira Apartments; she had a hat-check concession in a nightclub. Well ... He'd lend a helping hand to this woman who'd killed her child's spirit even before the child's body had been accidentally killed ...

Mrs. Blake returned to the room with an armful of Tony's clothes which she placed gently on a chair. Slowly she lifted up one of the child's garments and stared at it with troubled eyes.

"My little baby," she began weeping again. "God, tell me what *happened* to him! Tony, you're not gone ... It can't, it *can't* be true!"

Erskine choked back a wild and hot impulse to tell her what had happened. No; she'd never believe the simple truth, would she? And she'd wonder why he hadn't told before. Her tears unhinged him and he sat numbed and helpless.

"You mustn't give way, you know," he implored her.

Gradually she quieted a bit, then looked around with eyes swimming in tears. She rose and went to the sofa and picked up the crumpled copy of the *New York Times* and proceeded to spread it out and place the clothes on it. She was unfolding the second section when she paused and stared down intently at something that Erskine could not see.

"Look!" she called in a low, breathless voice.

"What?" he answered.

"It's *blood!*" she almost screamed, dropping the papers from her hands. "LOOK!"

Erskine ran to her side. The sheet of newspaper lay at her feet and he saw on it a huge, irregular blotch of what was undoubtedly blood; it had soaked through several layers of the newspaper and glared guiltily at him . . .

"That's blood; isn't it?" she asked in a whisper.

Erskine froze and did not answer; as he stared he recalled what had happened. While in the hallway, he'd been holding his newspaper in his right hand; but, after he'd returned from the balcony, he, without knowing it, had switched the papers into his wounded left hand. And, upon leaving Miss Brownell's door, he had had the idea of exchanging *her paper* for *his!* AND HE HADN'T REALIZED THAT HIS BLEEDING LEFT PALM HAD LEFT THIS TELLTALE BLOTCH OF BLOOD . . . Now, how could he explain that stain of blood? Each moment seemed to bring forth some incident to enforce his silence about the truth. Slowly, furtively, he secreted his taped left palm . . .

"That's blood," she said, talking more to herself than to him.

"Looks like it," he mumbled, not knowing what else to say.

"But . . ." Turning, she looked full at him. "Do you think Tony was *hurt* before he fell?"

"I don't know," he said.

"What happened to my child?" she wailed again, gritting her teeth in anguish.

He lifted the wad of newspaper, took it to the light, and made a pretense of examining it closely. What could he tell her? She'd take this bloody wad of newspaper to the police, unless he stalled her off somehow.

"Do you think someone bothered Tony?" she asked.

"It's hard to tell," he said. "He might have hurt himself, maybe—"

"But he'd have called me if he had," she insisted, her eyes blinking in bewilderment.

He had to think of something; yes; he had it...

"Oh," he pretended surprise. "I heard him crying this morning—"

"Crying?"

"Yes; I heard his drum; it woke me up ... Then I heard him crying in the hallway," he explained, actually visualizing what he was recounting. "I remember now; I went back to sleep, listening to his crying—"

"Then he was *hurt*," she said.

"Might've fallen off the hobbyhorse," he said with a hot and dry throat.

"But my paper was in front of my door," she said.

"Then he must have come into the hallway and tried to stop the blood with the newspaper," Erskine told her.

"But he ought to have called *me*," she protested, standing, her eyes wide with wonder.

"Maybe he thought you'd punish him," he argued.

His words had a tremendous effect upon her; she turned her face from him, sank upon the heap of clothes in the chair, and sobbed.

"Don't say that," she begged. "Mrs. Westerman tells everybody that Tony was scared of me ... No; no; no ... Tony, Tony, what did mummy do to you? I wasn't mean, Tony; Tony, my poor little helpless baaaby ..." She gulped. "I whipped him when he was bad, when he wouldn't obey ... But what else could I do?"

Erskine watched her like a hawk. Her sense of guilt and her grief were making her accept what he'd sug-

gested, but he knew that her mind would revert
again to this patch of blood and she'd be demanding
explanations. WHAT WAS HE TO DO WITH THIS
WOMAN? Stealthily, his left hand slipped into his
coat and touched the tip ends of his four pencils;
then he rammed the left hand into his trouser pocket;
she must not see the tape, white and glaring, that
covered the wound... With his right hand he
touched her shoulder.

"Don't get too worked up, dear," he told her. "I'm
sure Tony hurt himself some way, maybe worse
than he thought. Maybe that's why he fell..."

He led her to the sofa and she half fell upon it,
leaned forward and covered her face with her hands;
she sat like that a long time, sighing, trying to control
herself.

"Don't you think you ought to tell the police about
that blood on the paper?" he asked her; he had to
know what she was going to do.

"Oh, God, help me," she moaned, lifting her face
to him. "People say I'm bad... If I told about Tony
being hurt and scared to tell me, then that Mrs.
Westerman would crucify me. They'll believe anything she says... I don't know what to do."

She wept without restraint. He wanted to leave,
but fear would not let him. Suppose she changed her
mind and reported those bloody newspapers to the
police? If the police saw that his left hand was cut,
they'd want to know how it happened. And the most
casual test would prove that the blood on those
papers was of the same type that was in his veins.
He had to remain close to her now for his own
safety...

"Have you no friends?" he inquired softly.

"No," she breathed.

"I mean somebody with whom you can discuss all this?"

"I wouldn't dare tell the people I know how I live—"

"But don't you think we ought to show these bloody papers to the police?" he asked her again, boldly.

"What good would that do?" she asked despairingly. "It must've happened like you said; he hurt himself and was scared, *scared* of me ... And I don't want people to *talk* and *talk* about me!"

"Look, you must brace up ..."

She sat upright and stared stonily at the floor.

"I'm more alone than you can imagine," she confessed. Then, fearing that she was becoming too quickly intimate, she asked him: "Say, don't you want something?" She glanced down at herself. "Oh, God, I look a mess tonight ... Look, how about a drink?"

"No. Thank you."

"A cup of coffee, then?"

"Well, I'll take one with you."

"Good."

As she went into the kitchen, he watched the flowing movements of her body under the rose-colored robe. Her sheer animality gripped him with wonder. Listening to her bustling in the kitchen, he knew that he'd made, in spite of himself, an emotional commitment. But what was he to do with the woman? He didn't know her; he had to be careful. Maybe she was trying to trap him, preparing blackmail? Yet he sat, impatiently waiting for her return ... Why was he so glad to welcome her gestures of modesty, even though he thought her a whore? Why had her plea of ignorance put him so quickly at ease? She knew exactly, instinctively, how to put confidence in him. But was she doing it deliberately? And would she ever link that splotch of blood with him?

Suddenly a fearfully delicious idea declared itself in him: *one* act on his part could tie into a knot of meaning all of the contradictory impulses evoked in him by this dramatically sensual woman; *one* decision of his could allay his foolish guilt about Tony's strange death; *one* gesture of his could quell the riot of those returning memories from the dark bog of his childhood past; *one* deed of his could place him so near her that she'd never think of that damned spot of blood; *one* resolution could banish this precipice to which his retirement had brought him and set him down amidst a plain of days stretching out before him; *one* vow could enable him to answer God's call, save this woman, and serve Him as he should—*He'd ask her to marry him!*

It was an executive's decision—moral, clean-cut, efficient, practical; it hit the bull's eye of his emotions. It solved his problems, hers, squared little Tony's death, and placed him in the role of a missionary. His lips parted as the idea swam luminously in his consciousness. She'd obey him! she was simple; and, above all, he'd be the boss; he'd dominate her completely . . .

But, hadn't he once already rejected the idea of marrying her? Yes; but the situation was different now. He was in danger. And he need not really care what his friends would think . . . Hadn't he stood against them for years in his attitude toward religion? He'd marry her and take her to another city . . . He was not really guilty, but his marrying her would solve everything, banish all the shadows and make his world simple and concrete once more . . .

But how was he to go about this? He must make no blunders. It wouldn't be opportune to even hint at it now; he'd wait a little ... Ah! His waiting would be predicated upon his helping her arrange Tony's funeral; that would keep him near her. How wonderfully it all coincided! Not a single strand would dangle loose!

At last she came in with a tray filled with ham sandwiches, a pot of coffee, sugar, and cream.

"Oh, Mrs. Blake, you shouldn't've bothered, really—"

"But I haven't had a bite to eat today," she told him.

"I'm hungry too," he admitted.

"I'm Mabel," she murmured coyly, placing his cup of coffee on an end table next to his easy chair.

"And I'm Erskine," he said, smiling.

They ate in silence. Now that he'd decided to go all the way, he studied her. She was of medium height; her deep-set eyes were dark brown and held a remote, shy, impulsive look; her mouth was a little large without being in any way loose, with shapely, strong lips; but what excited him most were strong white teeth which, through her almost always slightly parted lips, could be seen hovering in her mouth, as though waiting to bite ...

"You know, Mabel," he began quietly, "I'm an insurance man. Only yesterday I retired after thirty years. I'm quite free and I'd be only too glad to handle the arrangements for Tony."

She paused with a mouthful of food, swallowed, and tears flooded her eyes.

"Oh, God," she sighed, "*would* you do that? I'm so *lost* ..."

"There, there," he consoled her, patting her arm, secretly glad of the firm but yielding flesh beneath the tips of his fingers.

Her face reflected humble admiration.

"You're *retired?*" she asked incredulously. "But you're so *young!*"

"I'm forty-three." He struggled to keep pride out of his voice.

"And I'm twenty-nine," she said absently. "But how could you retire so early?"

"I started work when I was thirteen."

She shook her head; she couldn't understand it.

"I began working when I was twelve, and I'm getting nowhere," she confessed.

He basked in the glory of the praise in her eyes.

"Tell me, what plans have you for Tony?"

"I hate to be such a bother."

"You're not. And I want to help. Really, I do."

"I'm not used to someone taking worries off my mind," she said wistfully. "It makes me a little scared."

"Why?"

"You're spoiling me," she smiled at him.

"Financially, are you able—?"

"I've a little money . . ." Her lips pouted sadly. "Since Mark, my husband, died—he was killed in the war—I've had to do everything alone. But it's *hard* . . . I was saving Mark's government insurance money to put Tony through college. Now, he's gone . . . And they're whispering that I neglected him. I'm just the butt of everybody's gossip. I didn't want Tony to grow up in New York, but my parents weren't able to help me with 'im—"

"Where do your parents live?"

"In Pennsylvania; a place called Altoona. I was born in Pittsburgh. My father's dead, but my mother's living. She's remarried. She and my step-father work—"

"Do you ever see your mother? Hear from her?"

"Not often," she admitted, blushing. "You see,

my life's so upside down, what with my working nights ... After twelve hours in that hot, smoky nightclub, all I'm fit for is to tumble into bed."

She gazed off somberly, her breasts hanging full under her robe. Watching her, his heart beat faster; then a counter-movement of his consciousness began as there rose before his eyes an image of what Tony called "fighting." Anger inhibited his swelling sense of desire. This woman bothered him: one moment she seemed so intimately close; the next moment she was in flight, captured by alien realities ... Who was this man who'd stayed with her last night?

"Do you ever think of changing your life, Mabel?" he asked her out of a mood of his brooding.

"What do you mean?" she asked; she was self-conscious, wary.

"Do you want to go on like this?"

"But what in the world can I do?" she wailed. She sulked. "I'm so tired of drifting." She sighed. "When I was married, things were simple."

Her helplessness lifted Erskine out of his fog of doubt. Yes; he could handle her ... She was begging for guidance.

"Do you ever go to church?"

"I used to, but I've no time now," she said.

"One learns to live by following moral laws," he said.

"Yes; I know," she said lamely.

She'd never had a chance and she'd be a willing pupil, and he'd cure her of her moral lapses. They talked in muted tones and she entrusted to him the full details of Tony's funeral and made out a check to cover the expenses.

"I'll take this burden off your poor shoulders, Mabel," he promised her.

"Oh, thank God for you, Erskine!"

"I'd better let you rest now," he said, rising. "I'm close by, you know. If you want or need anything, just holler."

"You're so kind—"

"It's nothing." A thought struck him. "Say, you didn't phone me today, did you?"

She seemed startled; her lips moved silently before she answered.

"Me?"

"Yes."

"Why, no. Why?"

"It's nothing. Forget it."

He squeezed her hand gently; in the doorway she told him good night as though she'd known him for a long time, and her face held an expression of innocent waiting.

But, when alone in his apartment, he was troubled. Did she still believe that she'd seen "naked feet dangling"? What did she really think of that stain of blood on the newspapers? And who was that woman who'd called and said that she'd seen what had happened? Yes; wouldn't being close to Mabel put that woman at a disadvantage? Later, he'd tell Mabel everything, he'd make her understand how it had happened . . .

But his doubts persisted. He yearned to believe that she was as innocent, as good as a boy believes his mother to be, but her manner told him that that was impossible. His desire for her was so close to his rejection of her that he couldn't separate the two. His mind was far too literal in its functioning to permit him to disentangle such conflicting emotions. Whenever he sought a compromise of his love-hate struggle, he grew distressed. He lay on his warm bed with wide eyes, staring until dawn; just before sunrise he fell into a fitful doze.

He awakened in a mood of calm soberness. How could he have felt such a headlong predilection for Mabel? He was so astonished at what he'd felt that it was like being told of the meandering emotions of someone vaguely known to him. Was it possible that he'd felt like that last night?

Hadn't he explained that spot of blood on the newspapers sufficiently for Mabel to forget it? And who'd believe her tale of "naked feet dangling"? Wasn't his fear of her unnecessary? But that phone call ... ? Mabel hadn't mentioned phoning him and he believed in her; she'd been distracting herself with her television set when he'd received that call. Who, then, was that woman? Mrs. Westerman? Why should she do that? She'd been in her basement apartment when Tony had fallen. Well, he'd wait and see if whoever it was that called would repeat their call. If they did, he'd go straight to the police.

As an insurance expert, he had some experience with the criminal mind. Now, if Mabel had seen "naked feet dangling," wouldn't she behave exactly as she was now behaving? She was a hatcheck girl in a nightclub and maybe she'd confided her story to some of her boy or girl friends? Wouldn't that account for the fact that his mysterious caller had not asked for a confirmation, had not waited for a reaction? He'd simply been warned that someone knew ... someone had seen him nude on the balcony ... But, if Mabel was in on this, wouldn't she be more concerned about avenging Tony's death? Certainly. She'd not call and say that she'd seen what had happened, and then do nothing about it. No; Mabel's reactions last night were genuine. Some outsider made that phone call, but for what purpose?

Then, after all was said and done, there was but one solution: his being close to Mabel would enable him to resist any attempt at blackmail, would allay any suspicions. He was fully awake now; an image of her weeping and writhing on the sofa brought him a sense of her body. He'd marry the girl; that would solve everything...

At eight o'clock Minnie, his maid, arrived, breathless, tearful.

"Mr. Fowler, is it true? What Mrs. Westerman told me about little Tony?" she asked.

"It's true, Minnie."

"Lord, have mercy on us all!" Minnie said, throwing up her hands. "But *how* did it happen?"

"I don't quite know," he replied uneasily. "He was playing and fell—"

"That poor little innocent thing," Minnie moaned. She sat, heaved a moment, then wiped her eyes. She rose, shaking her head. "That tyke needed a mother—"

"His mother was sleeping when it happened."

"Yeah. I know. She works at night," Minnie said. "She didn't have much time for that child...But she could've asked me; maybe I could've found someone to help her."

"It's too late now, Minnie. And I don't know if she could have afforded a maid. Oh, say, get me some coffee, will you?"

"Indeed I will, Mr. Fowler," Minnie said, trudging heavily into the kitchen.

Erskine was somewhat calmed by Minnie's naturalness. Why worry about some foolish woman's phoning when Minnie accepted Tony's death in so normal a manner? Erskine didn't believe that servants were quite human, but he felt that having them around brought one some standing; one could always depend upon them for simple, human reactions. And when Minnie brought him his coffee, he was grate-

ful for her level-headed sanity as she asked him
shyly:

"Mr. Fowler, don't you think I could make some
breakfast for that Mrs. Blake? Poor soul, she has no
one to look after her."

"I'll ask her," Erskine said, avidly appropriating
her suggestion. He found Mabel's number in the
phone book and dialed. "Mabel? This is Erskine
... Good morning?"

"Oh, good morning," Mabel said in a sleepy,
throaty voice.

"Did you sleep well?" he asked her; he was trying to picture how she looked in bed and his skin
tingled.

"I didn't sleep at all," she complained in a grum-
bling tone.

"Oh, dear! You've got to rest," he told her. "You
mustn't break down, you know. Look, my maid's
here. Do you want her to bring you some coffee?"

"I'd just love some," Mabel drawled in a thankful
voice. "You're sure it's no trouble?"

"None at all. And I'd like to talk to you for about
half an hour regarding arrangements for Tony,
hunh?"

"Sure. Come on over. God, you're wonderful to
me. I don't know what to say," she stammered.

"Don't say anything. Listen, I'm going to bring
you some sleeping pills. You've got to rest."

"Thanks, Erskine."

"See you."

" 'Bye."

He hung up. "Take her over something, Minnie,"
he said.

"I sure will," Minnie agreed heartily.

Erskine smiled and relaxed on his pillow. But a
moment later he was frowning. Why hadn't he

caught an echo of grief in her voice? She'd spoken as if she'd not lost her son! He wondered if perhaps she was not glad that Tony was dead... The idea made him flinch; he grew angry with himself for having such notions. The more he thought of Mabel the more he found himself unable to control the images that popped into his mind.

He drained his coffee cup, rolled out of bed, shaved, showered, dressed, and went out and rang Mabel's doorbell. He was surprised at the Mabel who opened the door. She was pert, brisk; she held a detached smile on her heavily rouged lips. Her body was sheathed in a tight-fitting, dark silk frock and a cigarette dangled from her lips. He entered her apartment feeling that her new mood was subtly shutting him out of her life. He fought down an attitude of resentment.

"Erskine, dear, how on earth will I ever be able to repay you for all your trouble?" Her voice indicated that she regretted having accepted his aid, that she'd reflected and thought better of the whole thing.

"But I've done nothing for you yet," he told her ardently. Maybe someone else had offered to help her? He felt that she was in flight, evading him. He handed her a tiny bottle. "Here are some sleeping pills. If you take two of them, you'll relax and sleep some."

"I don't know why you think of me," she said, taking the bottle reluctantly. "I'm so much trouble..."

As she led him down the hallway to the living room, he felt that it was her sense of inferiority that was making her so different. Her helplessness and gratitude rekindled his faith in her. Yes; he could handle her...

"Mabel, you must have faith and not fret so much," he tried to reassure her.

Her phone rang and she picked it up.

"Hello."

"   ..."

"Oh, Bill, dear! How are you? How sweet of you to think of calling me!"

Erskine was stunned at the change in her voice, which now purred with sensuality.

"   ..."

"Oh, I'm so-so ... A little tired."

"   ..."

"No; I'm sorry, Bill. I'm busy today."

"   ..."

"You mustn't say things like that to me!"

"   ..."

Mabel giggled.

"   ..."

"I just got out of bed."

"   ..."

"Okay. You'll call me later in the week, hunh?"

"   ..."

" 'Bye, now."

She hung up and turned to Erskine and smiled.

"An old friend," she murmured, her eyes shining. "Just a sec," she said and left the room.

Erskine fumed. What kind of a woman was this? She could turn her feelings on and off like a water faucet ... *Now, who was Bill?* And why hadn't she told him that Tony was dead? There'd been no overtone of sorrow in her voice at all. She's acting like the coldest fish I've ever seen! He was humiliated to feel that he was running her errands, but he'd *offered* to, hadn't he? But what really galled him was that another man was enjoying a relationship with her that he knew nothing about ... Couldn't she sense the impression she was making? Couldn't she feel the shocking impact of her actions? Yes; she was young; she hadn't enough experience to feel the weight of her behavior on the personalities of others.

She returned with a small suitcase.

"I must thank you for that wonderful breakfast you had your maid bring me," she told him, placing the suitcase on the floor at his feet and sitting next to him on the end of the sofa.

"It's nothing," he mumbled, trying to hide his resentment.

"Erskine, really, you mustn't run around like this for me, you know," she said, pouting charmingly. "Surely, you must have many more interesting things to do than—"

"It's absolutely no trouble, I assure you," he swore to her.

"These are Tony's clothes," she said, indicating the suitcase. "The undertaker asked for dark things, and I did my best."

"What about the burial date, flowers, music, and so forth?" Erskine launched forth as though he were back at Longevity Life sitting at his desk. "Just what do you want me to tell the undertaker?"

"What do you think I ought to say?" Mabel countered softly, throwing herself entirely upon his wisdom.

"But, dear, you must have some notion as to when you want him buried, the kind of coffin, and so on," he said.

"*You* tell him for me, won't you?" she asked him wailingly, on the verge of tears.

"But what kind of a service do you want?"

"Well, anything the undertaker says—"

"The ceremony ... When do you want it?" His anger seethed. "This afternoon? Tomorrow? Is that too soon?" he asked her bluntly. "You'll have to notify your relatives, your husband's relatives, won't you?"

"No. I have no relatives here in the city, Erskine," she said. "And Tony's father's people are in California. I want the ceremony simple—"

"Yes," Erskine agreed, fighting down his revulsion. *Doesn't she understand anything? This is no way to bury anybody* . . . "But haven't you notified Tony's father's people yet?"

"Not yet. I will . . . later. When I have time—"

"But, look here, Mabel," he said, wanting to slap her. "You're inviting some friends, aren't you? What about invitations?"

"I'm inviting no one," Mabel said, her face white and her eyes staring. "Just you, if you'll be so kind as to come, Erskine." Tears glistened on her long, dark eye-lashes. "You see, Erskine, I'm all alone in the world. I've no friends, really. I've no one I can really count on, that I can trust. I've nobody . . ." Her voice choked.

Erskine was stricken. His distrust and irritation fled. *Oh, God, what had he done to her? He'd judged her harshly a moment ago and now he hated himself.* Once more Mabel was redeemed in his feelings; once more she was the abandoned, tragic queen of his heart, a queen whom he'd serve loyally, without reserve. *She didn't even think enough of the other men she knew to invite them to the funeral* . . . Only *he* was being invited. He rose, took her hand and patted it.

"You can depend on me, Mabel," he said in a husky voice.

"You shouldn't bother about me," she whispered as she wept.

"Now, there—"

"I'm not worth it."

"Yes; you are worth it," he scolded her gently, tenderly. "And I don't want you to let me hear you talking like that again. Brace up. I'll attend to everything. Why don't you take a sleeping pill and get some rest?"

"I'll try."

"And I'll see you right after lunch, hunh?"

"Yes," she sniffed.

He picked up the suitcase and, after he'd let himself quietly into the hallway, he heard her phone ringing again. He paused, waiting, frowning, listening to Mabel's muffled voice through the door panels.

"Hello."

" . . . "

"Oh, Jack!"

" . . . "

"It's so good to hear your voice too."

" . . . "

"Oh, I'm all right. Just a little tired."

" . . . "

"No! I'm not working tonight."

" . . . "

"You *did?* How nice—"

" . . . "

"No; I won't be at the club this week. I'm really a little ill . . ."

" . . . "

"Darling . . . No; some other time, hunh?"

" . . . "

" 'Bye. Thanks for calling, dear."

Erskine was so angry that he wanted to fling the suitcase out of his hand. How had he gotten himself into this? He rode down in the elevator, asking himself: Now, who's Jack . . . ? And again he'd noticed that she'd said not one word about Tony's being dead. Didn't she care? "She's unnatural," he mut-

tered to himself. Why were all those men calling
her? Evidently, they'd been hoping to come and
see her. *What's she doing?* He felt nauseated. He
should be attending to his own affairs and not med-
dling with this cheap woman. She wasn't worth it ...

The tension that Mabel had induced in Erskine
reached a point of pain when he visited the funeral
parlor where a Mr. Jenkins, gray, unctuous, showing
a smile over a set of dead-white false teeth, told
him:
"Ah, good day, sir. You *are* Mr. Fowler, I believe?
The mother of the deceased phoned and said that
you were coming. Are you a relative, sir?"
"No. Just a friend."
Jenkins spread his white, withered hands softly
upon the air, lifted his eyebrows in a mechanical
expression of helplessness, and droned: "I want to
assure you, sir, that we've done our *very* best. The
poor child's head was terribly bashed in, I'm afraid.
We tried to make him as presentable as possible."
He caught Erskine's arm and squeezzed it sympathetically. "You must tell me if you think Mrs. Blake
will be satisfied." He piloted Erskine into a rear room
whose dim light made visibility difficult. Before
Erskine's eyes could adjust themselves to the shadows, Jenkins had approached a metal table and
pulled a heavy, white covering off a frail, waxen-
looking child whose flesh seemed almost translu-
cent. "You see, sir?" Jenkins said, pointing to the
child's head.
Erskine leaned forward, stared, and blinked.
"Is he Tony?" he asked.
"Oh, yes, sir. Was that the child's first name,
sir?"
"Yes."

"Yes, sir. It's Tony Blake, sir. Oh, forgive me, sir ..."

Before Erskine could object, Jenkins had pressed a button and a bluish glare of neon filled the room and Erskine saw that little Tony's face seemed much younger now and strangely at peace, as though in sleep. His lips were flexed in grim immobility; his hair, so much like Mabel's, curly and unruly, was slicked down over the left side of his forehead.

"You knew him, didn't you, sir?" Jenkins asked anxiously.

"Yes."

"Does it mar his features too much, sir?" Jenkins cocked his head, studying Tony. "We had to brush the hair over the wound, sir."

"I guess it's all right," Erskine mumbled, swallowing.

"His mother would know him, wouldn't she, sir?"

"I think so," Erskine said wearily.

Tears blurred his eyes and he was hearing Tony yell: *Bang! Bang! Bang! The Indians are coming!* And he remembered Tony asking in his high, lilting voice: *Do babies come from men and women fighting?* And he saw again the blank terror in those dark eyes floating atop the electric hobbyhorse and the mouth gaping open as the child went from sight, downward into space ... His throat tightened and he turned and walked into the reception room.

"I'm sorry, sir," Jenkins mumbled, following Erskine. "Just leave it to us, sir. We'll attend to everything. Tell me, when does she want the funeral, sir?"

"Will tomorrow be all right?" he asked timidly.

"Just as you say, sir. At 3 P.M., sir?"

"Yes."

"What denomination was the child, sir?"

"Just make it a simple, nondenominational, Protestant service."

"Very good, sir. With music, sir?"

"Yes. Organ music . . ."

"And a choir, sir?"

"No. No choir."

"Have you any special selections of sacred music in mind, sir?"

"No."

"Would half an hour of music be enough, sir?"

"I guess so."

"Are there any special effects you wish to have registered, sir?"

"Special effects?" Erskine asked, baffled.

"The mother wouldn't mind if we put the toy pistol in the child's hand, would she, sir?" Jenkins asked with a shadow of a smile. "He had his pistol in his right hand when they found him, they tell me. It makes him look so lifelike; don't you think, sir?"

"No; no . . . No special effects."

"Just as you say, sir."

Erskine stifled his anger. Mabel should have been with him; she should have told him what she wanted. Why had she dumped all of this upon him? He had half a mind to cancel the funeral, set it for another date, make new arrangements, etc.; but he cast the thought aside.

"How many guests are you inviting, sir?"

"Not many," Erskine hedged.

"Will fifty seats be enough, sir?"

"You'd better make it fifteen seats—"

"Will fifteen seats be enough, sir?"

"Oh, most certainly," he answered, unable to speak further. The truth was that even fifteen seats were too many . . .

He was edging toward the door in disgust. He

was afraid that Jenkins felt that he really did not care and he damned Mabel. He thinks I'm trying to get the child under the ground as soon as possible ... Coolly, he issued orders and arranged for Tony's body to be kept in a vault until Mabel could decide when and where she wanted the child buried.

"Now, sir ... I'd like your assistance in selecting a final bed," Jenkins told him. "Right this way, sir. It won't take but a second, sir."

Reluctantly he followed the man. Why was he doing this? He didn't know ... In a rear room were several children's caskets. Jenkins led him to a gray coffin lined with satin.

"Would this be appropriate, sir?"

"Yes," Erskine sighed, not really examining it.

"Very well, sir. That's all, sir."

Jenkins smiled whitely and shook Erskine's hand.

Enroute home, he told himself that he was a fool to help her. If she had come with him, he'd have stood at her side. No; no; no; no ... He *wouldn't*, *couldn't* marry her! He'd allowed himself to be swamped by pity; that was it. Her helpless state had blinded his judgment. He'd see this funeral through for Tony's sake and then he'd go to the police and tell his story and be quit of Mabel ... I'm running her errands and she's chatting over the phone with her boy friends ...

When Erskine's elevator arrived at the tenth floor of the Elmira Apartment Building, he got out and walked determinedly to Mabel's door and rang her bell. He rang three times and did not get a response. He was disconcerted. Maybe she'd taken all those sleeping pills and had passed out? Anything could happen to a woman like that, he thought in agitation. He rang once more; she surely was not in ... Grumpily, he let himself into his apartment.

Minnie came bustling in from the kitchen, wiping her wet hands on her apron.

"Mr. Fowler!" she called.

"Yes, Minnie?"

"Mrs. Blake told me to tell you that she's gone down to get her hair done," Minnie told him, her eyebrows arched.

"Oh, yes," he said, trying to hide his disgust.

"She said she'd be back soon."

"Thanks, Minnie."

"Your lunch'll be ready in a jiffy, Mr. Fowler," Minnie informed him.

Erskine grimaced. "I'm not hungry, Minnie. I don't want anything—"

"But you'll starve, Mr. Fowler!"

"I can't eat now, Minnie," he said irritably.

"I know," Minnie said softly, shaking her head. "You're grieving over Tony. But you oughta eat, Mr. Fowler . . ."

"I'll eat out later, maybe."

"Yes, sir."

He sat in his living room, near the open window, sunk in thought. What's wrong with me? he asked himself. Why was he letting himself get into such a state? Yet, he had to admit that he was frantic to know if Mabel had really gone to the beauty parlor . . . How could she think of her hair and nails when her son lay dead on a metal table under a blue neon light? Or had she gone to meet some man and had lied to Minnie? He didn't know which of these two possibilities he could have hated more . . .

A moment later he stiffened, hearing the low but distinct sound of Mabel laughing! She had come in and was talking on the phone! He went to his open window and tried to steal a glimpse, by leaning discreetly out and peering into her living room. Yes;

he could catch a slither of an image of her nyloned leg and a tan pump shoe swinging to and fro beyond the jamb of the living room door as she talked on the phone. He couldn't overhear the conversation but, occasionally, a low, contented chuckle wafted to him. *Hell!* He doubled his right fist, whirled back into the room, and smote the arm of his sofa.

"She's a whore!" he swore out loud.

"Sir?" Minnie's voice came from the kitchen.

"Nothing, Minnie," he muttered, looking about.

Minnie came to the door, her eyes round with subservience.

"You want something, sir?"

"No; no ... I was talking to myself, I guess."

Minnie vanished, looking puzzled. He'd ditch Mabel first thing tomorrow afternoon. *Damn her!* How could she laugh like that the day after her child was dead? And she'd never laughed like that with *him* ... He ran his fingers through his tousled hair. She was not thinking of him or Tony ... She was claimed elsewhere ... That cheap, cold monster!

He could not hear her laughter now. Ought he not to report his arrangements for Tony's funeral and tell her off? Then his mouth dropped open as he caught the metallic whir of a phone being dialed. Ah, she's calling *me* now ... He leaped up and stood before his phone and waited. But his phone did not ring. He glanced toward her window, trying to visualize what she was doing. Then there came to him again the sound of her throaty, laughing voice floating on the hot, humid air of the sweltering afternoon, —laughter that was like gurgling water tumbling over rocks in a meadow. She's phoning somebody else ... That *bitch!*

He threw himself full length upon his bed and closed his eyes, jamming his fist against his mouth, biting the knuckle. He had fallen into an attitude of waiting on her, of silent pleading with her, of begging for attention from her. But she kept on talking ... Yes; he'd have it out with her now! She must not think that he was a stupid, middle-aged man. He'd show her. He rose and went to her door and pushed the bell.

"Who is it?"

"Erskine!"

"Just a sec!"

She sounded too damned confident. He fidgeted, shifting from foot to foot. When she opened the door, he had expected to see her smiling; but her face, though rouged, was solemn, almost hard. She's acting, he thought with despair.

"Oh, hello, Erskine. Come in, won't you?"

"Hello," he said flatly, entering slowly.

She was newly coiffed, her eyelashes sharply defined, her fingernails freshly, brilliantly done. He walked heavily down the hallway, then paused, his eyes rounding. He could see a masculine shoe and a part of a trouser leg of a man sitting in the living room, near the door. Erskine was at once the proud gentleman.

"I beg your pardon. I didn't know you had company," he said stiffly. "I'll come back later—"

"Oh, no!" she said bluntly. "He's going."

A young man, bronze-skinned, twenty-four or thereabouts, with a crew haircut, a light tan tweed sports jacket, and a pipe in his mouth came into the hallway. He looked like he'd spent a great deal of time out of doors.

"Good afternoon," Erskine greeted him.

"How are you?" the young man nodded, speaking with offhand affability. He turned to Mabel. "Be seeing you, honey."

"Okay, Charles. You'll phone me?"

"Sure thing, kid."

" 'Bye."

"So long."

The young man was gone. Mabel closed the door and gave Erskine an artificial smile. He looked levelly at her, boiling with anger. He'd complete his errand and tell her off, so help him God!

"It'll be at three o'clock tomorrow afternoon," he told her abruptly. "It'll be a simple, nondenominational, Protestant service. I hope that's all right with you."

"Yes. How did Tony look, Erskine?" she asked; her lips were tremulous and her eyes misty.

"He looked all right," he said evasively, wanting to spare her. But why the hell should he? That was the trouble with this woman; she acted like an irresponsible child and the world was always sparing her some needful experience. "The undertaker was a little worried about the upper left-hand side of Tony's face. You know, where the skull was bashed in . . . Well, he combed and slicked his hair down over it; you can't see it . . . It changes his face a little . . ."

Mabel sank into a chair and held a handkerchief to her mouth and sobbed.

"I'll never understand *how* he fell," she gasped, her weeping stopping suddenly.

Erskine's left hand slipped inside his coat and touched the tips of his pencils . . . Was she thinking of those "naked feet dangling"? Or that bloody blotch on the newspapers?

"What did the police say about the railing?" he asked her.

"Nothing, so far . . ." She doubled her fists and rested one of them on each of her knees and frowned, glaring about. "I just can't get over the feeling that

Tony wasn't on that balcony *alone*..." She wept
again.

"Wasn't *alone?*" His fear returned hot and hard,
but the sight of her weeping calmed him down a
bit. She was closer to him when she wept; *this* was a
Mabel that that Charles didn't own...

"I don't know; I don't know," she mumbled.

"Who do you think could have been with him?
Another child?" he asked her.

"I don't know..."

"Maybe you just *thought* you saw somebody—"

"That's what Mrs. Westerman says."

"Did you speak to her today?"

"Yes. She hates me. She's gossiping about me..."

He recalled again that some man had spent the
night with her and his hate of her came again to
the fore. This woman... Yes; her shameless life had
killed her child! And she was too dumb, too sunk in
sin to be aware of it. Not only was she not worth
saving or helping, but she might eventually get
somebody to believe that she had seen "naked feet
dangling" on that balcony. And if that woman who'd
phoned should support her, the police would have
a case against him! They'd connect his wounded
hand with the bloody newspaper, and they'd want
to know why he'd not spoken out about what had
happened. A sense of guilt had kept him from speaking, and the longer he waited, the guiltier he became;
and the guiltier he was, the more difficult it was for
him to speak about it; his guilt had now become so
compounded, so involved that he doubted if he could
ever really speak...

He looked at her and, despite his hate, his senses
drank in the sensual appeal of her buxom, grief-
wracked body. The more distraught she seemed, the
more he wanted her; the more abandoned she was,

the more he yearned for her; and the more dangerous she loomed for him, the more he felt that he had to remain near her for his own self-protection. His desire for her merged with his hate and fear of her and he was jealous . . . He looked about for the pile of bloody newspapers and, when he did not see them, his uneasiness increased. What had she done with them?

"Who was the man who just left?" he heard himself asking.

"Hunh? What man . . . ? Oh, *him* . . . Charles; he's just a student. He comes to the *Red Moon,* where I work—"

"A friend of yours?"

"Nothing serious," she said simply, looking at him composedly.

"You like him?"

Her eyes grew troubled.

"Sort of."

"Did he know Tony?"

"No. He doesn't even know that I had a son."

"Oh!"

He was more baffled than ever.

"Why did he come here, then?" he asked her, knowing that he had no right to ask.

Mabel's face tensed. Involuntarily, her right hand flew to her bosom. There was a momentary struggle in her eyes, then she smiled; she seemed determined to be friendly.

"He missed me on the job and came by . . . Thought I was sick or something," she said.

"Why did you receive him?" he asked; his eyes looked off.

Her lips parted in astonishment. She had caught the drift of his questions.

"But he's just a boy," she protested, frowning at him, containing herself.

Could he ever believe anything she told him? He got to his feet and his lips formed a line of resolve. By God, he'd let her know right now what he thought of such loose, vile conduct!

"You mean that you didn't tell him about Tony?"

"No. Why should I?" she countered stoutly.

Erskine blinked. Maybe she knew a lot of things that she wasn't telling him ... At times this damned woman seemed so simple, so transparent; yet at other times she was so complicated, so full of shadows where no shadows had a right to be.

"That seems odd—"

"What's so *odd* about it?" she asked. "He's nothing to me. I don't want him in my life. He's a nice boy; he's a customer at the club, and—"

"Look, Mabel," Erskine confronted her. "Of course, I've absolutely no right to say anything to you about what you do. But don't you think you're acting kind of *hard* ... ? You just lost your *son* ... Don't you think it's more fitting, more seemly, to remain at home, and not see so many men?"

"But he's the only man who's come here, besides *you*," she said, her cheeks blazing. "And I had to get my hair done. I couldn't go to that funeral tomorrow looking like I was—"

"You could have told this boy who was here that you didn't feel well, that your son was dead, that you couldn't receive him today!" he shot at her.

"But he's nice!" she argued. "He comes to the *Red Moon* to drink—"

"But that doesn't give him the run of your house, does it?"

She stood and her face flamed scarlet.

"This is *my* house!" she screeched. "I receive whom

I please!" She sucked in her breath. "You *too?* Haven't I got enough trouble? My God, what do I *do?* What on earth do you think I'm doing with that boy? Making *love?*"

Erskine shuddered under the impact of her outspoken attack. It was precisely because he'd thought that *maybe* she'd been making love with Charles that he had accused her, but he had winced when she had put his thoughts into such hard, direct words.

"Why don't you leave me alone, if you think that I'm not good enough for you?" she cried. "Why do you and that Mrs. Westerman keep riding me? I didn't ask you to come here! You said that you wanted to help me! Now, I'm too low to be helped by you ... I told you I'm a hatcheck girl. Didn't I? Did I lie to you? God-dammit, I've got to *live!* What in God's name do you think I'm doing ... ?"

Should he believe her or not? Her shame and anger told him to believe her, but to whom could she be talking on the phone all the time?

"Who are these men who are calling you on the phone all the time?" he asked her; he was trembling with fear for trespassing into her life, but he had to know. "How many men are you in touch with right *now?*"

He had all but branded her a prostitute. She was still as stone, her eyes unblinkingly upon his face. Then she ran to the sofa and fell upon it, buried her face in her elbows and sobbed.

"No; no!" she screamed, turning and glaring at him. "Don't you talk to me like that! You *can't!* I can't stand it! What are you trying to *do* to me? I didn't ask you to come here! I didn't ask for your help! I didn't think *you'd* act like this ... What do you take me for? A whore?" As though the word "whore" had slipped out of her mouth unintentionally, against her will, she clapped her hands over her lips and moaned. "Leave me alone, leave me *alone*, I say," she sobbed, her shoulders hunched and heaving. "God, I want to die ... Oh, Mark, why did you die ... Oh, Mark, why did you die and leave me like this? I've no husband and every man wants to slap me ... Am I a criminal because I've no husband?" She bared her teeth in rage and knocked her fists against her head in a hysterical frenzy that shook her whole body.

Erskine was dumbfounded. Contrition gripped him. He went to her and stood over her. Had he reduced her to this? She was his again, nobody else's ... Pity welled in him so strong that he felt a weakness in his knees.

"Mabel ..." he said in a begging voice, almost a boy's voice.

"Go 'way," she cried. "Go 'way from me, you rich bastard! If you keep bothering me, I'll kill you, you hear?"

"Oh, Mabel, no!" he pleaded. "Let me explain—"

"Get out of my apartment!" she screamed.

"Mabel ... Listen ..." He reached out his hand to pat her shoulder.

"Don't you *touch* me!" she panted with fury.

He did touch her and she sprang to her feet, her eyes wild and bloodshot. "*Leave me alone!*" She was suddenly still, her eyes narrowing. "All right," she spat at him. "So what? Suppose I sleep with every man in this *block!* What it to you, hunh? What's it to anybody on this damned earth? It's *my* body, isn't it?"

"No, Mabel! God, no!" Erskine whispered, shaking his head.

"Suppose I'm selling myself, hunh? Do you want to

buy me? Then why don't you ask? Is that what's worrying you?" She sank to the floor, her hands clasped before her, unable, it seemed, to catch her breath. She appeared about to choke. Then she whimpered: "Tony, Tony, come back to mummy . . . Oh, God, tell me what *happened* . . . I'm so alone . . . Tony, you've gone and I don't want to live any more . . ." She tossed back her head, shut her eyes, and clutched with both hands at her hair and pulled as though trying to rip out the strands by their roots. She gasped and went into a spasm, her limbs trembling involuntarily; she seemed to have taken leave of her senses.

Erskine stood spellbound, appalled. Hot gratification suffused his body with so keen a sensation that he felt pain; he could scarcely breathe. She was his now, completely; like this, she belonged to him. He had conquered her, humbled her. He could now afford to be kind, to maintain his trust in her. Because she had been receding beyond his grasp, he had treated her abominably, had hurled at her his complaints and abuses and had checked her in her flight; but now he could be compassionate, loving towards her, for she was prostrate and at his feet . . .

"Mabel, dear, I'm sorry . . ."

She seemed not to hear him; her hands opened and shut with spasmodic rhythms and her eyes rolled so far back into her head that only the whites showed.

"Oh, God, she's fainting!"

He lifted her and carried her into her bedroom. Gently, he placed her upon her bed.

"Mabel!" he called in panic.

Her lips hung open and loose and she began to breathe a little easier. Ought he to call a doctor? Minnie? What had he done to her? Undecided, he watched her. At last her eyes rested unseeingly upon his face and the violent heaving of her bosom grew less. She turned away from him and stared dully off into a corner of the room, sighing in despair.

"Go 'way," she breathed.

"Mabel, forgive me ..."

"What are you doing to me?" she asked in a whimper.

"I'm sorry; I'm *so* sorry ..." he mumbled. What a fool he'd been to hurt her like this! She was, despite all her paint and sophistication, but a child and needed a child's loving care. He took her in his arms and held her tenderly close, whispering: "Forgive me, Mabel ... I didn't know ..."

"I thought you wanted to help me," she said; she was on the verge of tears again.

"I do; I do," he assured her.

Her body lay limp in his arms and he watched the tears drying on her long, dark eyelashes. How could there be any desire to deceive in anyone with a face so helpless and innocent as hers? Yes; he'd make it up to her. She was staring at him with a look compounded of accusation, entreaty, and despair.

"Erskine, why are you treating me like this?" she asked in a quiet, intimate voice. "What have I done to you?"

He hung his head. His right leg began to tremble. He felt something like a wave of heat flash through him and he tightened his arms about her. He wanted to hold this lovely woman who tortured him so and never let her go, wanted to hold onto her forever ... He bent to her and whispered:

"Mabel, I love you ..." He felt pleasantly dizzy, as though he were standing up high somewhere and looking down from a great height.

She turned swiftly in his arms, half lifting herself

on her elbow, and stared at him in utter disbelief.
Then she sighed.

"Erskine . . ." Her voice had a note of mild protest.

"I love you; I love you," he repeated. "I want to
marry you."

"No!"

"I mean it; I do—"

"My God," she said.

"I mean it honorably," he hastened to assure her.

"I don't know what's happening to me," Mabel said,
looking about vaguely, holding her head between the
palms of her hands.

"I love you; that's why I spoke to you as I did. I
couldn't help it . . ."

"But you don't *know* me—"

"I know I love you. You're haunting me. I can't
get you out of my mind, Mabel . . ."

Slowly she pulled free of him and sank into a chair
at the side of the bed, her lips hanging open in shock.
For a moment Erskine was afraid that she'd spring up
and run from him, accuse him of taking wanton advantage of her helplessness and grief, and he was
ready to let loose a net of pleas to stay her departure,
to beg her to forgive him. He felt his face burning
and he waited. She stared at the floor, then lifted
her large, dark eyes to his face. He saw a thousand
questions in them.

"I don't want to upset you, Mabel," he told her,
taking hold of her left hand with his right. "Perhaps
I shouldn't have spoken to you about my feelings at
a time like this. You're numb with sorrow. But you
were wondering why I dared criticize you, question
you . . . You must realize that I'm in love with you
and you seem to belong to me . . . Try to understand
that. I'm not much good at expressing myself, Mabel.
I'm a business man. I guess I'm just jealous. I can't

help it. Please, you mustn't think badly of me. Tell me, you don't, do you?"

Her eyes looked off and she did not answer.

"Please, I beg of you, Mabel," he pleaded, "don't be angry with me. Tell me that you are not angry . . ."

She still did not look at him or give any sign that she had heard. What was she thinking about?

"Mabel," he begged.

"Don't talk to me like that—"

"I must! Mabel—"

"I'm going crazy," she wailed.

"Mabel," he implored her.

"Yes," she whispered.

"Look at me . . ."

"No."

"Yes. Look at me, darling . . . You must *look* at me . . . I can't stand thinking that I've hurt you . . ."

He felt the slow, heavy thump of her heart under the silk dress, and again her eyes were wet, her lips trembling.

"Mabel, *look* at me . . ."

Slowly she turned her head and her eyes rested nakedly on his face; they were defenseless, those eyes, as they stared directly into his own.

"I love you," he said.

"Yes," she whispered and sighed.

"You're not angry . . . ?"

"No."

They were silent. He still held her hand; it was limp, warm, pliant . . . She sat in an attitude that made her seem bent forward, as under the weight of too much emotion. Her eyes, wet like a bird's wing caught in a rainstorm, went from his face and then to the floor several times. Then her body shook slowly with a slight motion that was scarely perceptible, shook each time her heart beat; she seemed to be, one second, leaning toward him, and then, the next second, leaning away ... He was afraid that she was about to collapse; he rose and enclosed her fully in his arms.

"I don't want to make things any harder for you," he whispered into her ear. "But do think of what I've said, won't you?"

She rested her head against his chest and closed her eyes. He had an impulse to kiss her, but he was afraid. A tremor went through him as the scent of her hair filled his nostrils. It seemed that she was surrendering to him, but he dared not risk interpreting her action in that light. He feared he would make her reject him forever.

"Think of what I've said," he entreated her. "Don't answer now. Think of it and we'll talk about it later, hunh?"

She nodded her head, then looked at him with an expression which he could not decipher.

"I'll go now," he said uneasily.

She said nothing; he took his arms from about her.

"Won't you have dinner with me tonight?" he asked her.

"If you want me to," she murmured.

He squeezed her hand.

"Until eight, then. Tonight?"

"Yes."

"I'll go now."

"Good bye, Erskine. You're so good."

"It's nothing. I want to do so much for you, Mabel."

He moved awkwardly toward the door. She rose and followed him, looking at the floor. In the doorway a Mona Lisa smile flittered across her lips, and it made Erskine wonder for a moment ...

"Good bye," he said.

" 'Bye."

He unlocked his door and went inside. He was trembling. It seemed that he was walking on air. He stood in the middle of the room and felt wrapped in the fulfillment of a long-sought dream. He smiled and, at the same time, a sense of dread made him bite his lips. Slowly he sank upon the side of his bed and gazed unseeingly about him; he was enthralled, elated, yet full of wonder and fear . . . He was glad that Minnie had finished her cleaning and had gone; if she saw him now, she'd think that he had gone out of his mind . . .

Mabel's phone rang, tinkling faintly through the afternoon's hot air. He rose and hurried to his open window, inclined his head, straining to listen, a deep frown dividing his eyes. He heard her voice, but could not make out her words. There came to his ears a low, rich, satisfied peal of laughter that ended abruptly, as though she were afraid that he'd hear her.

Who was she talking to now? *She's playing with me . . . !* That bitch . . . She didn't really care a fig about what he had said to her. Damn her! He grabbed hold of the pillow of the bed and, in a hot fury, balled it tightly in his long, strong hands, his fingers squeezing at the soft batch of feathers until the fingers of his left hand touched the fingers of his right, penetrating the fluffy bunch. Then his face flushed almost a black red and he ripped the pillow in two, tearing the cloth, and the white feathers scattered wildly in a dense, thick cloud about the room, floating and hovering slowly in the still, hot air. His rage was so deep that he could scarcely see.

Gradually he became aware that his left palm was throbbing with pain and when he looked at it he saw that he had torn off the patch of adhesive tape and drops of blood were pulsing and falling from the raw gash and forming a small pool on the highly polished hardwood floor. A large white feather floated slowly down to the puddle of blood, hovered above it for a second, then settled lightly upon its surface, its edges fluttering futilely, as though trying in vain to escape the clinging viscousness of the bright red liquid...

PART 3: ATTACK

We must obey the gods, whatever those gods are.
>
> —Euripides' *Orestes*

... This cup is the new testament in my blood; this do ye, as oft ye drink *it*, in remembrance of me.
>
> —St. Paul, *I Cor.* 11:25

See, see where Christ's blood streams in the firmament!
One drop would save my soul—
>
> —Christopher Marlowe's *Dr. Faustus*

STILL seething because of Mabel's flightiness, and suffering from the stabbing pain in his left palm, he mopped the blood from the floor, cleaned up the feathers, and rebandaged his hand with a thin strip of adhesive tape. He didn't want Mabel to see his wound when he ate dinner with her tonight...

His anger finally ebbed and he sat hunched, ashamed at how far he had let his emotions sweep him. What was wrong? It was plain that the woman was a simple slut; that's all ... All right. Okay. Why, then, didn't he forget her? But, even in asking the question, he knew that he couldn't leave her alone. Mabel was still his *agent provocateur* mysteriously inciting him, provoking him onwards towards—what deed? There were fleeting, frightening moments when he seemed on the verge of knowing just what she was silently urging him to do, and then the sense of it would suddenly elude him, would evaporate, leaving him anxious and perturbed. And at once, as though to protect himself against something which he had to know but didn't want to know, he'd remember that she knew something about those "naked feet dangling" on the balcony, that she was still puzzled over that blot of blood on the newspapers, and he'd suspect that she knew something about that phone call... It always seemed that he was ex-

169

pecting one kind of reaction from her and she kept bewildering him with actions that were completely contrary.

He was willing to forget whatever she had done in the past, but her past could not, *must* not follow her into his life. Hadn't she sense enough to know that? Didn't she know a good man when she saw one? At dinner tonight he'd be strict with her. She's just a little spoilt fool... And her prettiness has turned her silly...

Fatigued, he stretched upon his bed and fell into a sleep that was troubled by dreams. He thought that he was a child again and was in a huge and empty church which had row upon row of pews extending towards a tall pulpit and he was walking down the center aisle with slow and measured steps and to the sound of low, sad organ music and he was wondering why he was alone and walking like this and then suddenly he saw ahead of him a coffin beautifully wrought in shining silver and surrounded by heaping banks of flowers and as he neared the gleaming coffin something urgent compelled him to look down and he saw a dead woman who was lovely and young and lying in a flowing white muslin dress and it seemed that she was not really dead but just sleeping and then a strange man whom he felt that he had seen somewhere before but could not remember where came up to him from his left and the man's face was beginning to blur and he felt that the man was asking his permission to open the coffin so that he could see the entire body of the woman and the man reached forward with a hand clad in a white glove and slid down the lower half of the lid of the coffin and there lay revealed the lower half of the woman's body which was nude and he could see that her legs were moving slightly and then, by some strange power, the woman's body began to rot right before his eyes, rapidly, and the woman was turning an ashen color and then dark, the flesh falling away, crumbling, festering, melting, and finally resembling a blackened mass that shimmered and assumed the look of something slimy and wet and sticky and running, like tar, and it seemed that he was about to inhale the awful smell of putrefaction and he partially awakened, sweating, mumbling, sighing . . .

He opened his eyes at last, breathing heavily, feeling more fatigued than when he had lain down. Blinking, he saw that it had grown dark outside. He sat up quickly and turned on the light. It was seven-thirty. Oh, Lord! He'd promised to take Mabel to dinner. He pulled to his feet and took a shower, dressed, wool-gathering, all his fingers feeling like thumbs.

Promptly at eight o'clock he rang Mabel's bell, resolved that he'd be firm with her. After all, she'd not rejected his declaration of love, had in no wise indicated that it had displeased her. In fact, he suspected that she'd been not a little flattered. And, back of it all, he wondered uneasily just how far she would have let him go if he had insisted . . . He rang a second time, for she had not answered. She's out . . . Damn her! He was about to leave when his eyes caught sight of a slip of paper protruding from the jamb of the door, low down near the carpet. He took it and saw:

FOR MR. FOWLER

So! She'd written him a note. With grim face he opened it and read:

Dear Erskine: I'm sorry that I'm not in. Please forgive me. I'm with some very dear friends of mine. Won't you phone me at: ATWATER 9-0632? Just ask for Mabel ... We can fix a time for dinner and maybe you could pick me up, perhaps? My best—

MABEL

Why was she acting like this? Was she grieving over Tony at all? How could she so lightly accept another invitation? And only *four hours* ago he'd told her that he loved her? He oughtn't phone her; he'd teach her a lesson. He had some pride, hadn't he? Of course, she was with some Tom, Dick, or Harry, as always ... And, in the end, it was the necessity to know who that man was that made him decide to phone her. He'd swallow his pride for once. But she'd better not go too far; by Heaven, she'd better *not* ... He dialed the number and a man answered:
"Mike's Tavern! Mike speaking!"
He heard a din of babbling voices in the background. He tightened with jealousy. *She's in a bar!* My God! His hand shook. He wanted to hang up ...
"Hello! Who's on the phone?" the man's voice was rough.
"Is Mrs. Mabel Blake there?" he asked finally.
"Mabel Blake?"
"Yes."
"Hold on a second ..." There was a pause. Then: "Mabel! Mabel! Somebody tell Mabel she's wanted on the phone ... !"
Evidently she was well-known there.
"Hold on; she's coming."
He heard the receiver being laid down gently. He still wanted to hang up and, when he did hear Mabel's voice, he could not speak for a moment.

"Erskine, is that you, dear?"

He bit his lip and did not answer.

"Hello ... Is that you, Erskine?"

"Yes, Mabel," he dragged the words out of him.

"Oh, darling! I'm sorry ... Listen, do you want to come by here and pick me up? And I want you to meet some friends of mine."

"Where are you?"

"In Mike's Tavern. 50th and Sixth Avenue. Won't you come, honey?"

"But I thought we were having dinner together tonight?"

"We *are*, darling! I didn't forget. Oh, *do* come ... And forgive me for not being home when you came. But some friends asked me over for a drink; I was feeling so low, so lonely, so blue ... *Aren't* you coming?"

"All right, Mabel. I'll be there in quarter of an hour."

"Lovely."

"Good-bye."

He heard a smacking sound of lips over the wires and he knew that she was giving him a kiss ... Was she drunk? He hung up and felt like vomiting. Tonight he'd decide one way or the other. He hailed a taxi and slumped down in his seat to brood. Was it because he was old that her behavior seemed so odd? No; for thirty years he'd met and dealt with people of her age, but they'd been far more reasonable, honorable. Well, if she was really the kind of woman he was beginning to think she was, he'd tell her off. He felt bleak.

Erskine stepped with misgivings through the door of *Mike's Tavern* and moved forward through fumes of beer and clouds of blue smoke, searching for Mabel. There she was, sitting at a rear table surrounded by people . . . She was wearing a semi-evening dress and her face was sullen, heavy, her eyes slightly glazed.

"Mabel!" he called to her, unable to get any closer because of the crowd.

She looked about for him; when she saw him she let her mouth gape in a glad sign of welcome.

"Erskine, darling!" she crooned. "Come over here. Oh, darling, I thought you were angry with me and weren't coming . . . Say, you folks, move over and let Erskine in. Let him pass, won't you, Fred?"

"Sure thing," Fred agreed affably, rising and moving aside.

Erskine stepped beside her; he felt out of place, embarrassed.

"Share my chair, darling; won't you?" Mabel asked. "There's no other place to sit."

He sat next to her on one half of her chair and he smelt the alcohol on her breath. God, she's drunk . . .

"Erskine, meet Fred," Mabel said, waving her hand airily. She presented the others. "There's Will, Eva, Martin, Gloria, and Butch."

Erskine nodded to each of them and forced a smile.

"What'll you have to drink?" Fred asked Erskine.

"Just anything," Erskine mumbled, afraid to say that he didn't drink.

"Scotch and soda?" Fred asked.

"Sure," Erskine said impulsively. He felt that had he refused, it would have made him conspicuous, and he yearned to pass unnoticed among them . . .

Mabel caught hold of his chin and, holding it between her two palms, turned his face to her.

"I'm bad, hunh?"

"You're worried. Is that why you're drinking?" he asked her in a whisper.

"I'm bad; I know it," she said with exaggerated melancholy. "You left me alone and I didn't know what to do. My friends called me and I came ..."

"That's all right," Erskine lied; his face burned because she was demonstrating her intimacy too publicly by holding his cheeks like that. But he was determined not to lose his temper in the presence of her friends. He's have it out with her later.

"You're angry with me!" Mabel wailed and began a drunken kind of weeping. "Nobody likes me—"

"We *do* like you, Mabel," Will said, winking at Erskine.

"She's upset about something," Martin told Gloria.

"What can we do for her?" Eva asked of the table in general.

"Now, now," Erskine whispered chidingly to her. "Don't cry like that."

"I c-c-can't h-help it," Mabel sobbed.

"Give her another drink," Gloria said.

"Yeah; I want another drink," Mabel said, lifting her head suddenly and staring in front of her with tear-drenched eyes.

"Give Mabel another drink!" Gloria called to the waiter.

"Don't you think you've had enough?" Erskine asked her in a timid whisper.

"Now, don't you scold me, Erskine," Mabel said. "Be nice to me tonight, hunh? I need somebody to be nice to me ..." She was mumbling sentimentally. "Erskine, you're good ..."

The waiter brought Erskine's drink and Erskine took hold of the chilled glass, hoping that no one would notice that he did not know how to drink. With a quick gesture he lifted the glass to his lips and drained it in one swallow, struggling to keep a straight face against the sour sting of the alcohol.

"Do you want another one?" Fred asked Erskine, eyeing him curiously.

"Oh, no; thank you," Erskine said. "I've had a plenty."

"And where's my drink?" Mabel demanded, her head lolling.

"It's on the way; it's coming," Eva told her, smiling.

"And give Erskine another drink," Mabel said.

"I don't want another, dear," Erskine protested mildly.

"But you must have one for me, hunh, darling?" Mabel asked him in a begging tone.

"But, you know, I don't drink—"

"I don't mean *drink*," Mabel said. "Just take one for *me* . . ." Her face grew hard. "You've got to take one for me," she insisted. She looked at him with a sudden, drunken belligerence. "Do you think I *drink?*"

Erskine pretended not to hear.

"You won't answer? Tell me, Erskine," she demanded. "Do you think I drink?" She blinked back her tears. "I know . . . Mrs. Westerman's told you I drink . . . But I don't. I came here tonight because I'm sad, alone, and nobody really gives a good goddamn about me. Maybe not even *you* . . ."

"You're all right with us," Gloria told her lightly.

Erskine wondered if they were all making fun of him; he looked at Gloria and she smiled and winked at him. It suddenly occurred to him that they didn't really care how Mabel felt, that her state amused them more than anything else.

"You're mad with me, aren't you?" Mabel continued to hammer at him.

"No."

"Yes; you *are*," Mabel insisted. "I can *feel* it." She hung her head. "I'm not good enough for you—"

"No; don't say that."

"I *know* it," Mabel raged. She glared at him. "Say, what do you want with me, anyhow?"

"Aren't you hungry?" Erskine tried to evade her.

"What do you want with me, I asked you?" Mabel asked, her eyes sleepy and swimming.

"Aren't we having dinner together?" Erskine countered, seeking now to hurry the time of departure.

"Sure; sure . . . But we've got all night to eat in," Mabel said.

The waiter brought her her drink.

"We'll go after your drink, won't we?" Erskine asked with a note of pleading.

"Yes; I know . . . You wanna go . . ." Mabel waved her hand aimlessly, floating it limply through the air. "Awright, go . . . Just leave me here, like that . . ." She snapped her fingers. "Go then; I'll go to the dogs quietly . . . You don't wanna run? Why? You're free; go . . . No? Well, wait . . . wait, little man . . . If you don't wanna wait, then go . . ."

"You're drunk, Mabel," Fred said, winking at Erskine.

"Did I say I wasn't?" Mabel demanded. "And whose business is it if I'm drunk? I'm drunk because I'm blue—"

"All right," Gloria said, "be blue, then—"

"I gotta right to be blue," Mabel said proudly.

Erskine was tensely squeezing the fingers of his hands together, then he reached inside of his coat and touched the tips of the four pencils clipped to his pocket. Christ! His undershirt felt wet. The dense smoke was stinging his eyes and cutting his lungs. Disgust rolled through his veins. He longed to run from this, but could not. What puzzled him was that it was like a waking dream ... A flash of intuition went through him; yes, this woman was objectifying some fantasy of his own mind, just as he had objectified a fantasy in the mind of poor little Tony ... That was why Mabel held so powerful a hold over him. All right; all he had to do was rise and leave her and the dream would end. He blinked in confusion. But how could one act without knowing why one was acting? One simply couldn't get up and walk away from a group of people without giving rational explanations. He was ambushed in a morass of emotions far too complicated for his mind to untangle; so he remained, feeling uneasy. Another drink was set before him; he stared at it, dismayed.

"Everybody runs over me," Mabel was complaining.

"Why do you say that?" Erskine asked her.

"You *too*," she maintained.

"Take it easy, honey," Martin advised her.

Erskine suddenly lifted his glass and downed his drink. Mabel slapped him on the back and burst into a loud laugh.

"What's the matter?" he asked her.

"How you drink!" she yelled. "You are *funny!* Really, you *are!*"

He wanted to slap her, but he joined uneasily in the laughter that went around the table. Mabel rested her head affectionately on his shoulder, then she jerked her body upright.

"All right. You wanna go, don't you?" she asked.

"In a moment; finish your drink," Erskine said.

"Naw. You wanna go. Awright ... Let's go."

"Mabel," Erskine remonstrated, "let me pay for our drinks!"

"The drinks are on me, old man," Fred said.

"I shouldn't let you do that," Erskine said.

Erskine noticed that they all seemed fond of Mabel, but in a detached, impersonal sort of way. Before he came he had had the idea that he'd find some man hellbent for her body, but this loose, almost neutral atmosphere soothed him as much as it puzzled him.

Mabel stood, swaying drunkenly, her lips set in lines of sullen anger. Fred rose and Mabel squeezed past him and Erskine followed.

"Good night, everybody," he called self-consciously.

They smiled, waved, and said good night. Mabel now came toward him, her eyes directly on his face, her body veering uncertainly. He caught her arm and led her toward the door. A spot on his back seemed to burn red hot as he imagined many eyes staring at him; he yearned to turn and look, but dared not. On the sidewalk, he searched for a taxi, feeling Mabel's arm unsteady under the pressure of his hand.

"You didn't like my friends," she said.

He did not answer.

"Did you?" she insisted.

"I don't know, Mabel," he said. "How can I tell? I hardly know them—"

"You don't like 'em," she said with flat, drunken obstinacy. "I could *feel* it."

"I doubt if I've any feelings about them one way or the other," he lied cautiously.

"So, you're a snob, hunh?" she cut at him.

"Taxi!" he yelled.

"All right. You didn't like 'em . . . But they're damn good friends of mine, see?" she said.

"I understand," he said.

"You *don't* understand," she contradicted him.

A taxi swerved to the curb and they stepped in. "Chinatown, Mott Street," Erskine told the driver.

"They don't know Tony's dead," she said. "They don't even know I've got a son . . . *had* a son . . . Poor Tony! He's gone . . ."

Erskine was stunned.

"You never told them you had a son?"

"No."

"Why?"

"Why should I? It's none of their damned business, is it?"

Erskine could not answer that. Somehow it pleased him; it meant that she was really kind of pure. She kept the sacred part of her free from the profane, he tried to tell himself.

"Then, they're *really* not friends of yours, are they?"

"Sure they are," she said stoutly. "They'd do anything for me."

"But they don't know anything about you and you don't tell them anything—"

"I keep my life to myself," she said. "They don't tell me their personal lives."

"Oh, then they're just pals," he said.

Again he felt that she belonged to him. But she should not drink so . . .

"Is a Chinese restaurant all right with you?" he asked her.

"I don't care," she said, closing her eyes and leaning back in the taxi, her wan face an image of bleakness. Then, suddenly, she leaned forward and opened her eyes, staring downward at her feet.

"I'm no good, Erskine," she said.

"What do you mean?"

"We won't get along," she said. Tears began to

well in her eyes. "Let's be honest. Of course, I want to marry, but I'm no fool. I'm not for you—"

"Why do you say that?"

"You won't like me. You're lonely. You're retired. I just excite you; that's all." She sighed. "It'll pass . . ."

"But don't you want somebody to be excited about you?" he asked.

"Yes. But not in the way you are—"

"What's wrong with me?"

"I don't know." She shot him a glance. "I didn't say anything was wrong with you."

"No; no," he insisted in a sudden frenzy, "tell me, what's wrong!"

She stared at him. He saw a wisdom in her eyes that frightened him.

"Do you really want me?" she asked him slowly.

He winced when she put it in words like that; it offended him, made him feel that she was weighing him and finding him wanting.

"Yes," he said simply, but in the moment of his saying it, he felt that she had begun to recede from him again.

"Then why didn't you take me?" she asked him directly.

He was aghast. His projected emotions drained suddenly from her and she was a strange woman, a hostile one. So, that was why she had had that Mona Lisa smile on her face when he had left her at her door this afternoon . . .

"Why didn't you?" she kept after him.

"I don't know," he mumbled. She was beginning to seem like an enemy. Hate for her was coming to the surface again.

"You don't want me," she said.

"That depends—"

"On what?"

"On the *kind* of a person you want to be."

"You mean, on the kind of person I *am*—"

"No; no! It's what you *want* to be that counts."

"And how do you *want* me to be?" she demanded harshly.

"You could try to make people around you happy—"

"I do."

"*Do* you?"

"I try. Yes; I do; in my way."

"And what's *your* way?"

"I'm afraid that *my* way's not *your* way, Erskine," she said.

"And what's *your* way?" he kept doggedly at her.

"I'm a down-to-earth person. That's the way I am and I don't give a damn—"

"Do you realize that I've told you that I love you, that I want to marry you?"

"Yes. That's the strange part about it." She frowned.

"What's so strange about it? Tell me."

"I don't know. Oh, hell! Don't bother me ...!"

"Are you always like this?"

"I'm drunk. *Now*, I'm drunk. But I'm not *always* drunk."

There rose in Erskine's mind the scene of Tony's fear on the sidewalk, Tony's dropping his "fighting" planes, Tony's running and sobbing ...

"Did Tony ever see you drunk?" he asked her; his eyes were tense and hot.

For a split second she was sober; she turned and looked at him, then she burst into a loud and long laugh.

"What's so *funny?*" he asked; his teeth were on edge.

"*You!* This afternoon ... When you were angry

with me ... You reminded me so much of Tony ... *You and Tony ...*" She leaned toward him and touched his face. "You need a mother ..." Then she was sad. She covered her face with her hands in a gesture of convulsive grief. "Tony ... Tony ..." She wept. "Tony ... I want my baby ... Oh, Tony ..."

He put his arm about her and held her close. She wept all the way to Mott Street. Erskine did not know what to think or feel.

They picked and pecked at the Chinese dinner almost in silence, for neither of them was really hungry. To Erskine, Mabel was far off, almost objective, yet fatally linked to him. He felt cold, detached; and yet he could not tell or know how much of what he felt about her stemmed from his own feelings being projected out upon her or how much was being derived from her sheer womanness ...

"I'm tired," Mabel said.

"I'll take you home," he said.

In the taxi Mabel sulked. Erskine sat waiting for her to apologize for her behavior.

"What're you thinking, Erskine?" she asked.

"Nothing," he lied.

"I know. You're angry with me."

"No."

"You are. You just don't want to admit it. Hell, I shouldn't have let you say what you did to me!"

"You regret it?"

"Yes."

"Why?"

"We're *too* different. I'm not for you. I'm nothing, nobody."

It touched him; she was veering close to him again, demeaning herself, surrendering her independence and throwing herself upon his judgment. She was pliant, raw stuff of feminine material which he could mold and exalt as he pleased.

"Mabel, we must get to know each other more and—"

"No. The more you know of me, the less you'll like me."

"Not necessarily."

When they were in front of her apartment door, Mabel gave him her key and, just as he turned the key in the lock, Mabel's phone rang. She rushed breathlessly forward and Erskine stood staring at her, again cut loose from her . . . Yes; some man was phoning her . . .

"Just a sec, dear," Mabel called to him as she picked up the receiver.

Erskine watched Mabel's face light up; her heavy manner changed to one of light-heartedness.

". . . but I've been busy, Kent," Mable was explaining.

". . ."

"No; I can't. Tomorrow afternoon I'm busy—"

". . ."

"You did! What is it? A Buick?"

". . ."

"Oh, I'd *love* it, Kent!"

". . ."

"But not tonight."

". . ."

"Call me next week, hunh, Kent?"

". . ."

"You're silly, Kent!"

Mabel giggled. Erskine's mind was made up. He'd not even wait to say good night or good-bye. The whole thing was ridiculous, degrading . . . Just as he went out of the door, he glanced back and saw Mabel waving her hand at him, indicating that she

ID:R0102469667
813.52 WRIGHT
Savage holiday : a no
Wright, Richard, 1908
    route to: ADULT
in transit to:
    WEST E
HOLD FOR:
D008906357
PASSMORE JERMAINE L

11/23/2005,10:22

wanted him to remain, but he went resolutely out. This was the end. He knew exactly what to do to terminate this farce.

In his living room, he placed a sheet of his personal stationery on his desk, took out his fountain pen, and wrote in a clear, flowing hand:

Dear Mabel:

You must realize now, as surely as I do, that what has happened between us is a sad mistake. This entire thing is a foolish case of mistaken identity and, if we let it continue, it will only mean misery for the both of us. Upon myself I willingly take the full blame, and I only beg, with all my heart, your indulgence and forgiveness. I freely confess that I was wrong in my hot-headed scolding of you; I had no right to do it. It was indefensible on my part. But I ask you to understand under what stress of emotion I was when I did it. Mabel, it might just be that you see and know all of this much more clearly than I do. In fact, from what you said to me tonight, I think you do. So, please try to forget and forgive what I was impulsive enough to say to you this afternoon.

Believe me when I say that I do want, for the sake of our common memory of dear little Tony, to help you and be your staunch friend. But, beyond that, I now realize that there is no place for me in your life. And you are far, far from understanding the kind of man I am.

I shall see you tomorrow afternoon at two-thirty for the service. Don't hesitate to let me know if you need anything. I shall be hurt if you want my help and do not ask for it.

With all my best,
Sincerely,
ERSKINE

He folded it, stepped into the hallway and slipped it under the sill of her door. A vast weight seemed to lift itself from his tensed muscles, yet, as it did so, he was conscious of a sense of looseness, of desolation, a feeling of having been abandoned upon some rocky ledge of some cold, bleak mountain. He undressed and got into bed, assuring himself that he had done the wisest thing, that he would have gone crazy if he had kept running after that wild girl . . . She's just a plain tart . . .

But he couldn't sleep. What had he done? What had he solved? Mabel, if she was determined, could still make trouble for him with her story of the "naked feet dangling" . . . And there were those bloody newspapers . . . And who was that woman who'd called him? And didn't he have a duty to let Mabel know somehow just what harm she'd done to little Tony? His mind wrestled with the question of why he was constantly changing his attitude toward her. Why did he love her one moment and hate her the next? Slowly he began to realize that he hadn't been honest with himself, that his motive in writing that letter was to hurt Mabel, to jolt her loose from whatever men she knew. Would it? Suppose she agreed to what he had said in the letter? The thought distressed him. He tossed restlessly on his bed in the dark, his lips moving soundlessly as they followed his thoughts. Ah, hell, why had he ever dared to talk to her in the first place? If he had kept to himself after Tony had fallen, why everything would have been all right . . .

The silence of the night hours weighed on him. Had she found the letter? She'd gone to bed, no doubt. The hell with it! He'd go to the police in the morning and tell his story and then he'd leave New York tomorrow night . . . A good vacation was what he needed; it'd get all of this churning rot out of his system ... Yes; a good sea trip ...

His phone rang. Ah, she was phoning him ... He'd known that she would ... He'd bet that she was feeling properly chastened ... A tight smile hovered on his lips as he picked up the receiver.

"Hello," he said.

The line hummed softly and there was no response.

"Hello, hello, hello ..."

He heard the receiver click and the line went dead. Erskine stood, sweat coming again on his face. Had that been Mabel or had it been the other woman who'd called him twice before? Then he heard his doorbell ring. He hesitated, debating. He had the sensation that some huge, invisible trap was closing slowly over him. Perhaps it was Mabel ... He opened the door and it was Mabel, silent, solemn, her features washed clean of rouge and powder; she was wearing her rose-colored nylon robe.

"I want to talk to you, Erskine." She snapped out her words.

"Come in," he said, tying his own robe tighter about his waist.

She entered and he closed the door. She walked slowly down the hallway, looking around. Finally she entered his bedroom. He followed her, sat on the edge of his bed, watched her, waited for her to speak.

"Erskine, what in hell's the matter with you?" she asked abruptly and in a tone of voice that he'd never heard her use before.

"I think I expressed myself pretty clearly in my letter," he said. In vain he tried to stifle a sense of dread that was now seizing hold of him.

Mabel took her cigarettes from the pocket of her robe and popped one of them into her mouth and

lit it. Inhaling deeply, she let the twin spirals of
smoke eddy from her nostrils. He waited, hiding his
wounded left hand; several times Mabel seemed on
the verge of speaking, but she checked herself.
Finally she launched forth in a matter-of-fact tone:

"Look here ... Yesterday you came to see me of
your own free will and offered me your help. I
was lost, scared, alone, at my wit's end and I accepted what you offered me. Then, out of the blue,
you floored me by criticizing me, bawling me out,
calling me almost a prostitute or something ... And
you did that when you knew damn well that I was
shaky and nervous from what had happened to Tony,
and yet you did it ... Then when I demanded to
know why you dared do it, you told me that you
loved me and wanted to marry me ... You said that
you were sorry and you begged me to forgive you
... All I wanted you to do was to get out and leave
me alone, but you insisted. Now, all this happens
within ten hours. But now, all of a sudden, you are
saying that you take it all back, that it was all a mistake ... Now, what in hell does all this mean, Erskine? What in hell do you want from me? Why are
you bothering me? What have I done to you? What
are you so upset about? Why are you hanging around
me, all on edge, on pins, watching me like a
hawk ... ?" She filled her lungs to get her breath.

"The way you act—"

"What in hell do you *mean?*" she flared.

"These men—"

"What in hell's that to *you?*" she shot at him. "If
you don't like the way I'm living, then leave me ...
But stop bothering me!" She sank into a chair.

"I had a right to expect a reasonable response to
my declaration—"

"All right," she snapped. "You didn't get it. So

what? I'm all upset about Tony and you come to me talking about love, love, love ... It was Tony I was responsible for, not *you* ... I don't know what *happened* to Tony. I've been pounding my brains to find out what to do about it, and you start pressing me about loving me ... Do you call *that* responsibility?"

Her attack was so frontal that his feelings shriveled. My God, what a hell cat! If his emotions could have been represented by an image of reality, that image would have been of a pile of hunched muscles crouched in self-defense, ready to spring and attack that which was seeking to destroy it. Mabel's words made leap to life in him two opposing sets of bars, as it were: bars that had kept him propped to a stance of religious rectitude, and bars that had shut out all the past that his love and need of religion had been designed to deny.

"Mabel, I'm jealous," he confessed in a confused, weak voice.

"But you don't *know* me, so how can you be jealous?" she asked him. "You don't know my friends, and when you meet them, you don't like them. Tonight you sat like a lump on a log, itching to get away—"

"I wasn't so much jealous of *them*," he muttered.

"Then what are you jealous of?"

"*You!*"

"But what have I *done?*" she cried. "Ask me anything you want to ... I'll tell you. I'm no angel, but I'm not what you seem to be thinking. Oh, hell! I don't *understand* you."

"It's *you*," he told her again, his eyes fastened upon her face.

"You don't want me to speak to my friends over the phone? You want me to remain in your sight every

minute of the day or night? Why? Don't you have
any trust at all in *anybody?*" she asked.

He did not reply. He stared guiltily at the floor.
There was silence. The air became charged. Each
seemed to be waiting for the other to speak. And
each passing moment made the tension all the greater. Erskine perhaps could have sat for eternity without feeling sure enough of what he felt to say a word.
And if that silence could have prevailed, Erskine
eventually would have been able to find another sort
of prison in which to live, another set of duties to
fill his life, to keep him from that vast, complex
world which resided in his body and which he called
himself and which he'd never met and didn't want
to meet. If silence could have reigned, he'd have
mastered himself again by being his own jailer, his
judge, his own warden . . . But Erskine was being
called to meet himself.

"Erskine, just why did you come to me?" she
asked. "We've lived next door to each other for
three years. You've said good morning and good
evening, but you never so much as looked at me.
Why now?"

"Hunh?" Erskine grunted; he felt cornered.

"What do you *want* from me?" she insisted.

"I've told you—"

"No; no . . . You're fighting me in some strange
way. What have I done to you to make you fight
me? There's something back of all this. Something's
worrying you, something you want to tell me . . .
What is it?"

"Why do you ask me that?" he asked; his hands
were trembling.

"I *feel* it—"

"What makes you feel that?" he asked quietly.

He dared not look at her and his nerves were taut as he waited for her to answer.

"It's in everything you say and do ... When you're with me, you're not thinking of *me* ... What are you thinking of?"

Panic rose in him. How much did she know or suspect? Did she have someone waiting outside the door? Or was she alone in this attack? The more she tried to get at his heart, the more he hated and feared her.

"Mabel, what are you getting at?" he tried to fence her off.

She rose and stood looking down at him.

"Erskine, do you want to confess something to me?" she asked gently, quietly.

His head jerked up and he stared at her, his lips moving soundlessly.

"*Confess? What?*" he asked finally.

"If you want to confess, then only *you* would know what—"

"What do you think I want to say, Mabel?" he asked her in a breathless sort of way. He knew that there was but one thing that she could be thinking of, and that was Tony. Really, he was wanting her to bring it up; he was hungry for her to ask him. Her asking him would release him from this nightmare ...

She sighed; her face was concentrated; she sat on the bed beside him. He could detect no anger in her and it baffled him. She caught hold of his shoulder and turned him round.

"Is it about Tony? It's about Tony, isn't it?" she asked, nodding her head affirmatively.

He did not, could not answer; he could scarcely breathe.

"What about Tony?" she kept at him. "You know something; I can feel it..."

He leaped to his feet and pointed an accusing finger at her, determined to blast her for her dirty sensuality; he wanted to hurl his charge at her but, when his words came out, they were mild, defensive, and deflected from their target.

"*You* called me just now, didn't you? And you hung up the phone without saying anything... Isn't that true?"

"Yes," she said, nodding. She didn't take her eyes off him.

Oh, God! She knows; she *knows!* He could see it in her face. But he was certain that she had no real proof. He couldn't exactly explain how, but he was positive that she'd called him those other two times also...

"Why did you hang up the phone?"

"I wanted to talk to you face to face," she said.

Again he wanted to come straight to the point, but he could not. He was dying to know for certain if it was she who'd called him twice before.

"What were you asking me about Tony?" he asked her, avoiding her eyes, hating himself, wondering how he could ever tell her.

Mabel looked at him out of the corners of her eyes and gave a silent laugh. She crushed out the stub of her cigarette and lit another.

"I wish to God I could make you out," she mumbled, shaking her head. "You've been tracking me down like a detective. All right, Erskine... Listen, I know that you know I didn't love Tony. I didn't want 'im. You knew that, didn't you?" she asked him quietly. "But why in hell does it mean so much to you?"

He was thunderstruck; she was naming her own crime!

"I felt it; yes ... But why didn't you love him, want him? He was your own son, your child," he stammered.

"Because it's not in my nature to be a mother," she told him with stark simplicity. "I met Tony's father just before he went overseas. The last night I spent with him, which was the night we married, he said he wanted to come back to a child of his ... It was crazy. I let him do it. Then he went and got himself killed. What the hell! I didn't even get any fun out of it. Suddenly a baby is dropped in my lap, and I've got to work—"

"But that's no excuse for neglecting him!" he arraigned her.

"I did the best I could for Tony," she said, but there was no sorrow in her voice. "I worked nights, slept days ... What could I do?"

He felt words on the tip of his tongue; he wanted to know definitely that it was she who'd called him those other two times. He felt that it was foolish and wild of him to be so centered upon that, but he was compelled to ask, even if his asking incriminated him.

"Mabel, you called me *twice* before, didn't you? You called once and hung up ... Then you called again and said—" He broke off in confusion.

"Yes, I called *both* times," she said with satisfaction. "I was wondering when you were going to ask me about *that* ..."

"But why did you call *me?*"

"I felt you knew something. I was trying to bluff you into telling me—"

Was she trying to trick him into admitting something? She hadn't been in her apartment... And her television had been going...

"But you didn't call me from your room, did you?"

"No," she said and smiled. "But how do you know that? I called from the outside... I left my television set going... I was worried sick, I went for a walk... I called once from a newsstand. The second time I called from a bar. I knew you were worrying about that. But how could you know that I wasn't in my room when I called?"

He didn't answer; he couldn't tell her that he'd been spying into her room. He'd trapped himself. *She knew now that he knew something about how Tony had died!* What a cold monster of a woman! She's been watching and studying me all along...

"Erskine?"

"Yes."

"What happened to Tony?" she begged, pleaded.

"What do you mean?" he snarled; his body was hot as fire.

"How did he die? Did he fall? Did someone push him?" She touched his shoulder. "I ask you that because you've asked me if I thought that; you've asked me that *twice*... How did blood get on my newspaper? Did that have anything to do with Tony? Did you see what happened?"

"Why do you ask *me*? How should *I* know?" he tried to stall her off.

"Was that you, your naked feet, I saw dangling on that balcony?" she asked him directly at last.

Heat flooded his brain. It was out in the open between them. But why had she waited so long to accuse him?

"You saw—?"

"Not what really happened; no... Not all of it. I

knew that something was happening, but I didn't
think it was serious ... And I didn't think you were
involved in it ... I went back to sleep. I didn't see
Tony fall ... I thought he was still on the balcony.
I was standing and looking out of my kitchen window. I was afraid that Tony's drum would keep
people awake. I waved at him to keep quiet; he
nodded to let me know that he'd obey ... He kept
so quiet that a little later I went out into the hallway to see about 'im; he was all right ... But the
next time I looked, I didn't see him; I was about to
leave the window when I saw two feet, naked feet,
dangling in air and they went up, *up* and out of
sight ... I'd swear that it was *your* balcony. Erskine,
what on *earth* was that? Do you know?"

Erskine buried his face in his hands. Yes; he should
have told his story before now. But, yes ... Only
one person had seen him, only *one* person had phoned
him, only *one* person had known about that bloody
newspaper ... And that person was Mabel, and she
sat six inches from him ...

"Why do you think I had anything to do with it?"
he asked her, lifting his head and speaking in a
whisper. He had hoped that his question would be
defiant but, as he spoke, he realized that it was almost a confession.

"Because nobody else wants to speak to me about
it," she said promptly. "They accepted the police
story; they think that Tony just fell, that I neglected
him ... Only *you* kept hanging around me, accusing
me ..." She frowned. "Did that person whose feet
I saw ... ? Did he go into your apartment, Erskine?
What was happening?"

"Are you trying to say that *I* killed Tony?" he
asked with rough anger.

"I'm asking you to tell me what happened, if

you know," she insisted. "And I think you do know . . . If you don't tell me, then *what* am I to think? I'm not accusing you; I'm not threatening . . . Erskine, I'm asking . . . I thought of telling the police and asking them to ask you, but that Mrs. Westerman was going to be a witness against me, talk about me . . . Then suddenly you came to me of your own accord . . ."

Erskine knew now that he was in danger; Mabel's mentioning the police made him leap to his feet and confront her.

"It was *you* who killed your own child!" he shouted in fury.

Mabel stared, blinked. She bit her lips in concentrated thought.

"Are you crazy?" she gasped. "What are you talking about? You're *hiding* something . . . A man as wealthy as you are, why do you stoop to this?" She looked nervously about the room. "I want a drink . . ."

"There's a bottle on the shelf in the kitchen," he said. "I keep it there for others; I don't drink."

She kept her eyes on him until she went out of the door. He heard her getting the bottle, opening it, and pouring herself some whiskey.

"Do you want a drink?" she called to him.

"Hunh?" He licked his lips nervously. "Yes," he whispered in despair.

He needed one. She brought him a tumbler half full and placed it in his hand. She was watching him closely. He lifted the glass and drained it. She sat the bottle of whiskey on the floor.

"God," she said, "that's no way to drink—"

"Why?" he asked innocently.

"You just sip it. It'll knock you out if you don't," she explained, studying him with a frown.

"I don't drink," he mumbled, coughing.

"Oh, you drink all right," she said. Then, reflectively: "Say, maybe you oughtn't to drink, if you drink like that."

"I'm all right."

She sat again and held her glass. He saw that a part of her robe had fallen off her crossed legs, leaving a bare strip of thigh showing. He kept his eyes on the floor.

"Let's get back to Tony," she said after taking a sip out of her glass. "Tony's dead. I'm sorry ... But he was an awful burden to me. I admit it. But I had nothing to do with his falling ... I'd gotten in at four o'clock and was dead tired, and then his yelling wouldn't let me sleep. Erskine, I'm no mother. How could I be a mother and work nights in a nightclub? I'm not complaining or excusing myself. It's just the way things are; that's all ... I was always trying to think of what to do with Tony. I knew I wasn't doing what I should. I wanted to put him in a home, but he got hysterical and wouldn't go. So I kept him. But I never would've killed 'im. Now, why do you say that I did?"

He wanted to reach out and slap her; instead, he sat heavily upon the bed.

"You've got some reason for saying that I killed 'im," she went on. She sucked deeply on her cigarette. "Erskine, did you bother Tony in some way?"

"What in God's name do you mean?" he demanded, knowing full well what she meant.

"Did you frighten Tony in some way?"

"Only in the way *you* frightened him," he muttered, rising and turning from her.

"I don't get you. What are you talking about? Why do you keep accusing me?"

Erskine felt that now was the time to tell her. He was trembling. By God, he'd tell her ...

"Erskine, look, I'm not accusing you of anything. But if you know anything, tell me . . ."

"Are you hinting at blackmail?" he demanded, glaring at her.

She reddened with shock.

"What would I blackmail you *about?*" she countered. "I hadn't thought of *anything* like that. But was that why you offered to marry me? To keep me silent? To cover up something? To make it impossible for me to suspect anything about *you?*" Her eyelids fluttered as she thought. "Say, how *did* that blood get on my newspaper? You didn't want me to tell that to the police! I remember now! You tried to make me believe that Tony had hurt himself, that everybody knew that Tony was scared of me—"

"You are *glad* that Tony's dead!" he thundered at her.

"I'm not," she defended herself quietly. "But why are you trying so hard to make me guilty of something? I'm still waiting for you to tell me what *happened!* And I've been waiting all along . . . Instead, you got cold feet and told me that you loved me . . . Were you going to marry me to keep from telling me?"

He came to her, nodding his head affirmatively, and demanded: "How much money do you want?"

"I'm not asking you for anything," she said, speaking without rancor or surprise.

"But you *were* going to marry me, weren't you?"

"Frankly, I doubt it," she said, pouring herself another drink. "But why are you accusing me of killing Tony, Erskine? Don't try to wriggle out of answering . . ."

"You brought Tony up in a way that made him scared of certain things," Erskine said sheepishly, hesitantly.

"What on *earth* are you saying?" Her mouth hung open.

Her right leg was bare to the thigh now and he could see the tip of the nipple of one of her breasts, and he knew that she was utterly unaware of it.

"You had no damned business having a child," he growled savagely.

"That may well be," she agreed readily.

"It was because Tony had seen you as you are *now*, and perhaps in a worse state, that he fell," Erskine explained.

"What do you mean? Drunk?"

"NO. NAKED!" he screamed at her, thrusting his face within a few inches of hers.

"*Naked?*" she repeated the word wonderingly, shrinking from him.

"Yes. *Naked...*"

She glanced down at herself, then hastily drew her robe together.

"Like this?" she asked, then bent forward and burst into a loud laugh. "Are you *stupid?* You're *funny*, really!"

"He saw more than *that*," Erskine snarled, waving his finger in her face.

"What in hell are you talking about?" she demanded, her face growing pale with anger.

He paced to and fro, then whirled on her, his hate breaking forth in a torrent of words to lash at her, to humble her, to break her down so that he could love her, master her, have his say-so about her. As he talked his face flamed a dark red and he banged both of his fists repeatedly on the top of his dresser.

"Mabel!" he shouted. "By God, I'm going to make you understand this, even if it's the last thing you'll ever understand on this earth, see? YOU KILLED

TONY! How? Like this ... You had let Tony see you naked many times, naked and making love to men, *many men ... Tony told me so!* I swear it! That poor child couldn't understand what he saw. You were so careless, so stupid, so inhuman, so brutal that you thought that a child could look right at such as that without its influencing him! How *could* you do that? Tony didn't understand what was happening when you let him see you making love to men ... Maybe you were too drunk to care—I don't know. But Tony thought the men were *fighting* you ... And you'll never understand how scared he was of that ... He thought of it night and day; he dreamed about it; he tried to find out what it meant; he lived in terror of it ... He couldn't interpret it in terms that made sense to him. It was just a picture of violence, violence for no reason that he could accept or understand ... I swear to you that this is true, Mabel. Your son was terrified of naked people, naked men in particular ... You made him feel that if he ever saw a naked man, he had to run for his life ... for he didn't want that violence, that *fighting* to happen to him ... Tony told me that he didn't even want to grow up to be a man, because he felt that he'd have to *fight*—he called it *fighting!*—women like his mother ... Mabel, you crushed that child; you killed him even before he fell from that balcony ... Aw, you sneer at me, huh?

"But, listen ... That morning I tried to get my Sunday paper from the hallway, see? I was naked. I was about to take a shower. I opened my door to pick up the paper and the door slammed shut in my face and I was locked out. I didn't know what to do. I was terrified, embarrassed ... Naked, I rode down in the elevator to try to get hold of Westerman and ask him to unlock my door ... But there

were too many people about ... Then I thought of
climbing back into my apartment through my bathroom window ... I ran to the balcony ... Before I
knew it, I was there and Tony was looking at me
... He went white in the face ... He was *scared,
scared* ... It all happened so quickly that I didn't
have time to think of what to do or say ... He was
standing on top of his hobbyhorse, and he fell, thinking that something was about to happen to him ...
He thought that I was going to *fight* him ... Understand? *I didn't touch Tony, so help me God!* I didn't
say *one* word to him, and I swear it! The whole
thing happened in ten seconds or less ... What Tony
had seen you do, and he'd seen you do it *many*
times, made him frightened and he fell; trying to
run, he fell; trying to keep what he'd seen happen to
you from happening to him, he fell ...

"He tried to grab hold of that iron railing ... I was
leaning against that railing; I'd fallen against it. That
damned hobbyhorse was leaning against the railing
too. Then Tony, in falling from the hobbyhorse, tried
to grab that railing to save himself. *That* was what
pulled that railing out of the wall ... Now, do you
understand? Have you got sense enough, understanding enough, imagination enough to know what
you've done?" Erskine's face was contorted with fury
and flecks of foam stood at the corners of his lips.

Mabel's eyes were riveted upon his face. She was
completely rattled. The total picture had been presented too brutally and suddenly for her to grasp
it. Red blotches appeared on the skin of her face
and throat. Then, suddenly, the general sense of it
struck her and she jumped to her feet.

"You sonofabitch!" she screamed. "My God ... It's
that Mrs. Westerman who's got your head all twisted
... Why, I was *alone* when Tony fell ... I'd had

some company; yes...A friend of mine saw me home; but he'd gone...Tony wasn't even in the room when my friend was there—"

"No; no...you stupid fool! You're so sunk in muck that you can't understand *anything* any more! I'm talking about what Tony saw you do *before* that morning! *Many* times and *many* mornings before that!"

Mabel's face suddenly seemed washed of its humanity. She sprang forward like a tigress and her lips curled in fury.

"You can't say that to me!" she screamed.

She hurled her glass at him; it missed his head and smashed against the wall behind him, shattering and sending a shower of whiskey over the room. Then she leaped at him and sent her open palm smacking against his undefended face.

"You dirty little whore!" Erskine roared.

He swung his fist and struck her on the shoulder; the force of the blow spun her round and she sprawled on the floor. For a second she was still, stunned. Then she began to weep.

"I'll kill you," she sobbed. "You sonofabitch! You killed my child and now you're trying to kill me..."

Clumsily, she clambered to her feet, clutching blindly at her robe which was sliding off her body.

"I'm going to report *all* of this to the police," she panted. "You're a pervert of some kind...You won't get away..."

She fumbled with her robe. Erskine's eyes were like cat's eyes as he watched her. Then he advanced upon her with doubled fists. She backed off, terror masking her face. She crumpled to her knees, her robe falling open. In that moment she was his again. He was still, watching her. She crouched against a wall, her nude body trembling, her hands lifted to defend herself. Erskine relented, staring down at her trembling terror.

"Don't hurt me; don't hurt me, please," she whimpered.

Yes. She was humble now ... His tension slackened a bit. She'd been in flight from him, but his words had halted her and now she lay huddled against the wall, her naked body shivering, her lips begging for mercy.

"Mabel ... I'm sorry. I didn't mean to hit you," he gasped. "Listen, let's talk about this ..." He went toward her.

She stared at him without understanding; she thought that he was advancing to strike her again and she sprang, losing her robe completely. Feeling her nakedness, she stopped suddenly, looked down at herself in bleak dismay, clamped her knees together and covered her breasts with her spread fingers. Her mouth gaped to scream, but when she spoke, her voice was a stammered weeping:

"Don't hurt me; don't hurt me ..."

"Mabel ... Listen, for God's sake! Try to listen ..."

"What are you doing to me?" she whimpered.

"Listen ... Don't be scared." He got her robe and flung it to her. "Put it on."

With palsied movements she got awkwardly into her robe, watching him; her face was like that of a terrified child.

"Sit down," he said. "God knows, I never hit a woman before in all my life ... I'm sorry." He covered his face with his hands.

She didn't know what to do. She glanced at the door, then back to his face. She was trying to read his mind, then she seemed to decide to trust him once more. She sighed.

"Sit down; sit down, Mabel," he begged her. "I won't hurt you . . ."

She edged toward a chair and sat. He backed off till his legs touched his bed; then he sank upon it, closed his eyes and rocked his head.

"Good God, Mabel," he groaned. "We're both at fault in this . . . Be calm and try to understand. Please . . . There's no sense in being wild. What's happened has happened . . . That's all. But we can try to understand what happened." He lifted his eyes pleadingly to her. "The first thing to try to understand is that I'm telling you the truth about what happened to Tony . . . All right; I'm a damn fool for not telling what had happened in the first place . . . I was foolish! But it was such a freakish accident, such a silly accident that I was in a funk . . . I didn't want to tell anybody about it. I-I thought t-they wouldn't believe m-me . . . The last thing on earth I expected was for my door to slam shut in my face and lock me out, naked in that hallway . . ."

They both stared unseeingly toward each other in silence.

"Your door slammed . . . ?" she asked at last in a timid voice; she looked at him, then off, frowning.

"Yes; I was locked out, naked . . . I couldn't even break the door down—"

"Did your door slam very loud when it shut?" she asked.

"Like a rifle shot—"

"What time was that?"

"A little after seven-thirty; nearly eight, I think—"

"Then *that's* what I heard," she said wonderingly. "I thought that was Tony . . . It woke me up."

The muscles of Erskine's face relaxed a little.

"Oh, thank God, you can understand maybe . . . Try to understand *something* . . . Be honest with

yourself, Mabel. Look at this for what it simply *is*,"
he begged her. "What killed poor Tony is what
both of us did to him ... Which of us is really responsible, who knows? All right; I am upon the balcony ... But how could I know that Tony would
react so?"

"Why didn't you knock at my door?" she asked,
her eyes round with the effort to comprehend.

His eyes grew sullen and he frowned. He bent forward and rested his elbows on his knees and cupped
his chin in his hands.

"I didn't dare, Mabel," he confessed. "I didn't
know you ... And I didn't think about it. I was trying to dodge everybody ... And I was wild, crazy,
scared ... What does one do in situations like that?"

"Yes; *you* wouldn't think of doing a little simple
thing like that," she said and even managed a slow,
rueful smile. "You're very moral ..." She shook her
head. "You and Tony ... You say you talked to Tony
about this ... ?"

"He talked to me—"

"Oh, God, it's all so sad and true it makes me
sick," she moaned.

"Be honest and try to understand ..."

She lifted her head with a quick jerk.

"But why on earth didn't you call Tony and tell
him to get Westerman—?"

A tremor went through Erskine. He doubled his
fists and jammed them against his eyes.

"Christ, I forgot that the child was on that balcony!" he exclaimed in horror. "I heard 'im earlier,
then he got quiet and I forgot 'im."

"Good God," Mabel breathed. "Could such a thing
happen?"

"It *happened!*" he swore fervently. "I pray for you
to believe me; I beg you with all my heart ... What

do you want me to do to prove it? Look, Mabel, I'm
so glad that all of this is out in the open at last.
Keeping my mouth shut about this was like having
a hot poker rammed in my heart! Listen, Mabel,
let's you and I go right now to the police station
and tell them what happened ... Let's go and tell
them everything. Right *now!*"

Mabel moaned and closed her eyes.

"God, Erskine, what good on earth would that do
now?" she asked in a hopeless whisper. "I'd die on
the spot if you told the police what you told me
tonight ... I'd die of shame." She choked.

"But what ought we to do?" Erskine asked.

"Tony's gone," she wailed. "What did I do to my
baby ...?"

She caught hold of the hem of her robe and
pressed it against her mouth in a gesture of convulsive grief, then she leaned forward in her chair. Her
dark eyes were pits of fear as she lifted them slowly
to Erskine's face.

"D-do you t-think that he w-was scared of ...
scared of *that,* Erskine?" she asked in a broken voice.

"Yes, Mabel," he told her. "Tony was alone, *alone*
in a world he didn't understand. He saw danger
everywhere, even where there was no danger ... Did
you know that he was even afraid to play with his
toys?"

"Afraid of his toys?" She gulped. "Oh, God, Mrs.
Westerman told me something about that once, but
I didn't believe her ... I thought she was trying to
insult me. Jesus, I shouldn't have had a child ... I'm
no mother ..." She keened: "He was scared of his
little toys ..."

"He could hardly play with them, Mabel," Erskine explained sadly and gently. "He'd get scared

and run off ... Oh, I can't explain it all, Mabel. Tony was obsessed with fear about everything. He didn't understand what he saw you do, and he got it mixed up with things that didn't have anything to do with it ... Even his little airplanes were men and women *fighting* to make babies ... At times he was so frightened of them that he couldn't touch them."

They were silent. Mabel sat, crushed. Beyond the window it was black night and a slight wind made the curtains tremble. The small clock on Erskine's night table ticked loudly in the still room.

"Mabel," Erskine called plaintively to her.

She opened her eyes and stared at him; there was only wonder, fear, pity, humility and a kind of dread in her now. He felt that she was his, only his now ... He rose and went slowly to her and touched her shoulder. He thought that his breath would stop when her hand lifted itself and, hesitantly and tenderly, covered his own. He took her in his arms; he found himself weeping.

"I don't understand anything any more," she whispered through a dry throat. "What did I do to my child?"

"May God help you," he told her. "Little Tony's gone ... I'll do anything on this earth to try to make it up to you."

They clung together, weeping.

"Mabel?"

"Yes?"

"I still love you," he said. "Make any condition you want. I'll accept it and abide by it. I'm in your hands. We both must go to the police and tell them about Tony ..."

"No; no; no," she cried, shutting her eyes.

"But I want to marry you, Mabel," he said. "I need you ..."

He felt her body shudder slightly in his arms.

"But I'm not for you, Erskine," she whispered compassionately.

"Let me decide that," he begged her.

"Are you sure you want me, Erskine?"

"I'm *sure*," he said, looking into her eyes with tears in his own. "Are you engaged to anyone?"

"No."

"Then you'll marry me? There can be no question of my hiding or covering up something now," he argued. "We both know what happened and now we're free from *that* ... You'll marry me?"

"But, Erskine, we're so *different*," she protested weakly, shaking her head.

"Look, I'll change some and you'll change some," he said, figuring it all out neatly. "Tell me: will you marry me? Tell me *now* ..."

"You really want it?"

"I do, with all my heart. Now, tell me ... Will you?"

She began weeping afresh.

"Tell me; tell me," he implored her, squeezing her shoulders.

"Yes; yes, Erskine," she sighed.

He crushed her to him. "We'll make up for little Tony, won't we? We may have a son, hunh? We'll have something around which to build a joyful and solemn relationship, hunh? You understand?"

"Yes," she whispered. "And I need somebody ..."

She threw her arms about him and clung to him.

"Erskine, teach me how to live, won't you?" she asked him. "I'm through; I'm licked ... You'll teach me, tell me what's right?"

"Yes, yes," he assured her.

She lowered her eyes and then started violently. "What's the matter?" he asked.

"What's that?" she asked. "Your hand ... It's bleed-ing ... God, blood's running on my arm ..."

Erskine saw that the bandage on his left palm had worked loose and that the gash was pulsing red, staining Mabel's arm.

"I cut myself," he mumbled.

"How did you do that?"

"I was climbing through the bathroom window," he told her. "I ripped my hand on a corner of the sill."

"Oh," she breathed. She gazed off, then she turned and looked questioningly at him.

He knew that she was now connecting that bloody patch on the newspapers with the bleeding wound on his palm.

"Mabel," he began in humble tones, "I lied to you about that blood on your newspaper ... I made that stain ... And I was too scared to tell you ..."

"But how? When?"

Erskine sighed, avoiding her eyes.

"I was holding my newspaper in my hand when they took you down to see Tony," he explained. "I know I ought to have spoken up then, ought to have told the truth ... But I couldn't, just couldn't ... One moment I was ready to tell, then the next I'd think of what people would say if I told how it had happened ... You see, I just couldn't believe that anybody'd believe me ..."

"Oh, God!" she exclaimed.

"I switched your paper for mine, because mine was all crumpled," he went on doggedly. "I didn't think that you'd look at yours; I thought you were too worried to bother about the paper, and you'd throw it away ... Mabel, it was a cowardly thing to do. Now, you have the whole truth. Do you believe me?"

Her eyes deepened with pity as she gazed at him. A ghost of a sad smile flitted across her wan lips.

"You and Tony," she said with a sigh. "Come here; let me wash that blood off your hand..."

She caught his arm and led him to the bathroom and washed his hand and bound it securely with tape.

"I said that I needed somebody," she said. "But, by God, I think you need somebody, too."

He caught her and kissed her for the first time.

"Mabel," he murmured.

"Erskine," she whispered. "You're really so silly, like a boy..."

"We'll redeem everything, won't we, honey?"

"Yes."

"Our love will be a monument to Tony..."

"Yes." She grew thoughtful. "Erskine, what about your family and friends? Would you acknowledge me before them?"

"I want you in spite of them," he said. "If they don't accept you, they reject me. I'm with you; understand?"

"Yes."

The phone in Mabel's apartment began to ring, the sound coming clear and sharp through the night air, through Erskine's opened window. Mabel cocked her head.

"That's my phone," she said in a voice that was suddenly matter-of-fact, practical.

He hugged her closer, frantically.

"Mabel," he whispered.

"My phone's ringing," she said, trying to disengage herself.

"Let it ring..."

"But that's Harry," she protested. "I must answer that..."

His face went white. She pulled herself out of his arms; his hand clutched involuntarily at the sleeve of her robe and, as she went from him, the robe slid from her body and she stood naked before him.

"Give me my robe," she said with tense impatience. "I must answer the phone."

The phone was still ringing.

"No; no . . . Let it ring," he insisted. He still held her robe. "What do we care about who's calling?"

"But, Erskine?"

He seized her nude body and held her close to him.

The phone rang once more, then fell silent. She turned and stared at him with a strange expression on her face.

"You *are* jealous," she said in amazement.

"Yes," he admitted shamefacedly.

"But how could we ever live together?" she asked in open wonder.

"We'd be together," he muttered.

"Not all the time," she said. "There are things that you must do, and there are things that I must do. We couldn't be together every minute . . ."

"But you'd be faithful to me, wouldn't you?" he asked her.

She stared, smiled a ghost of a smile, and looked off.

"If I were *married* to you, yes," she said cryptically.

"Why 'if,' Mabel?" His frown was dividing his forehead now.

"Listen, Erskine, if two people are married and are satisfied with each other, they are faithful," she explained.

Erskine was tortured. A moment ago he had felt that he had her forever, and now he was not so sure. She was fleeing from him again. He was feeling abandoned, naked, lost . . .

"And if you were dissatisfied with me, you'd b-b-be unfaithful, wouldn't you?" he asked.

She did not answer.

"Mabel," he called to her in a heavy voice. She was a stranger to him now. She loomed as the personification of an enemy.

"Yes."

"You've had many men, haven't you?"

She pulled away from him. Her face was chalk white.

"No; tell me," he insisted, speaking through his teeth. He attempted to take hold of her hand, but she snatched it beyond his reach. She grabbed her robe and flung it on.

"*Tell me,*" he all but threatened her.

A flicker of fear went over her eyes as she stared at him.

"I'm not asking you about what women *you've* had," she said. "So, why are you asking me this—?"

"I've got to know," he said stubbornly.

"I'm not married now," she said evasively.

"Ah . . . So you're free for everybody, hunh?" he cut at her. "Is *that* it? But if you were married to me, you'd be faithful to me, wouldn't you?"

"If you were faithful to me; yes," she countered ironically.

Erskine gritted his teeth. Why wouldn't she come clean with him? Why did she forever hover agonizingly beyond his reach?

"How many men are sleeping with you now," he demanded to know.

"Goddamn you!" she blazed. "You can go straight to hell!" She started for the door.

He grabbed her arm. If he lost her now, it was for always . . .

"No; no; you can't go now!" he told her.

"You turn me *loose!*" she said, twisting and trying to evade him.

"Mabel, *talk* to me..." There was a mixture of threat and pleading in his voice. He despaired of making her know how serious he was.

"I'm tired," she moaned suddenly, wilting. "Listen, Erskine, all of this is *impossible*...I can't marry you. We'd never get along. I don't understand you..."

"Are you sleeping with this Harry?" he questioned her in a low, tense voice.

"No."

"What about that fellow called Jack?"

"Good God! Leave me *alone!*" she yelled at him.

"And if I married you, you'd say the same damn thing, wouldn't you?" He spoke through clenched teeth. "You'd *never* tell me the truth! I'd never know where you were..."

She wrenched herself free, her eyes wide with fear and hysteria.

"You're crazy!" she shouted. "I'll never marry a man like you...You'd drive me out of my mind! What's the matter with you?" She began a high-pitched, choking kind of laugh that stopped quickly, then she looked at him with cold detachment. "Listen, I sleep with whom I damn please. I'm a woman; I'm free...What the hell's the matter with you? Why do you keep on prying into me? Your mind works in a strange way... Really! What do you want to find out about me?"

"I've found out what I want to know—"

"Erskine, there's something wrong with you," she said soberly. "Maybe we ought to go to the police station, after all. You've told me so many lies that

I can't tell what you've done . . . By God, I'm going to report you—"

"You stinking bitch," he said. The expression on his face was distorted, mobile.

"To hell with you," she snapped, her hand reaching for the doorknob.

He lunged at her and she shrank away, flinging out her arms to protect her face, her robe falling open and loose about her. Erskine stood over her like a waiting cat. She lifted her head and lowered her hands to look at him. In that split second Erskine's flexed fingers flew to her throat. She screamed.

"No! You're hur—!"

Her voice died in her chest. He forced her to the floor, screaming: "You're no damned good!"

She twisted from him and ran, nude, to the opposite wall. When he came at her this time she screamed again and ran into the kitchen. She flicked on the light and stood nude amid the white refrigerator, the white gas stove, the gleaming sink, the white-topped table. He followed her. She put the table between them, her mouth open. Erskine's long arm shot across the table and his flexed fingers seized her throat once more. He snatched her brutally forward, bending her naked body backward over the table. She was fighting desperately now, clawing frantically at his hands that were trying to strangle the breath from her panting throat. Once again she succeeded in pulling herself partially free and tried to scream again. Erskine then brought his right fist down hard on the side of her head and she lay with glazed eyes, moaning:

"Oh, God, don't kill me . . . God, help me . . ."

Erskine glared about, then he snatched open the drawer of the kitchen table and drew out a long butcher knife with a stainless steel blade and a plastic handle. She raised her head and looked at him with eyes of terror.

"No, no, no ... " she was whispering, her breath issuing through her nostrils.

As she opened her mouth to scream, he brought the knife down hard into her nude stomach and her scream turned into a long groan.

With machinelike motion, Erskine lifted the butcher knife and plunged it into her stomach again and again. Each time the long blade sank into her, her knees doubled up by reflex action. He continued to hack into her midriff and, from the two-inch slits which appeared in the flesh of her abdomen, blood began to run and spurt. Her breathing was heavy, as though she was trying to catch her breath. Huge drops of sweat popped out upon Erskine's face; his lips were flexed. He stabbed her over and over and he did not cease until his arm grew so tired that it began to ache. Her knees no longer jumped now; her legs had stretched out and hung downward from the table, swinging a little. Her lips moved wordlessly, as though trying to form pleas for which there was not enough air in her lungs to give sound ... Her house slippers had fallen off her feet and lay on the white-tiled floor. Her blood was running from her body to the table top, and drops began to splash on the shining tiles.

Erskine stepped back from the table and lifted his eyes. Daylight stood in the room; dawn showed white through the windows and Erskine's hand, which still gripped the bloody knife, fell limply to his side and his breath came and went in his chest with a wild, sobbing sound. He stared at the sprawled, bloody body on the table, as though amazed to find it still there, yet knowing that it had to be there, that he'd killed her. He heard the sound of blood dripping into pools that had began to form on the floor. He started away from the table, then turned back and tossed the bloody butcher knife carelessly on top of the slashed and bleeding stomach.

With slow feet, as in a dream, he walked into the bathroom and stared at his white and sweaty face in the mirror above the washbowl, and he seemed dully surprised to find that the face he saw was still his own...

...he was looking in the mirror to see how bad he was, for his mother had said: "Go and look in the mirror at yourself and see how bad you are!" And he was looking at his face and the face he saw was his own and it wasn't bad...His mother had lied to him. He hadn't changed; he could see no bad in his face...

Yesterday he had been playing with the little girl next door—Gladys was her name—and he had taken her little doll and had "killed" it and had told Gladys that the doll was his mother and he had "killed" her because all the boys had said that his mother was bad...

He had taken a dirty brick bat and had beaten the doll's head in, had crushed it and had told Gladys: "There's my mama....I killed her; I killed her 'cause she's a bad woman..."

And Gladys had cried and had told her mother and Gladys' mother had told his mother and his mother had asked him if he'd said it and he'd refused to answer. And his mother had said: "Look in the mirror and see how bad you are!" And now he was staring at his face in the mirror and it was his own face and it had not changed...

For perhaps five minutes Erskine stood before the mirror in the bathroom staring at his face which evoked that dimly remembered, far-off scene. Then he felt sick; he bent over the commode and vomited. He leaned against the wall, breathing heavily. Finally he washed the blood from his hands and dried them. He paused in the bathroom door, staring into the kitchen with a kind of sullen, stolid pride at the nude, bloody body stretched on the table. Huge, gleaming pools of red blood had now formed on the tiled floor.

He dressed and stood glowering into space. He went to the open window and looked out at New York stretching glitteringly in the bright Tuesday morning sunshine. He turned with sudden purpose and went out of his door, rode down in the elevator, and walked four blocks west and entered a police station. He saw a policeman reading a newspaper behind a tall black desk. He walked slowly up to him and placed both of his hands on top of the wooden railing.

"I want to see the officer in charge," he said in a clear, distinct voice.

"That's me. What can I do for you?" the policeman asked, lowering his newspaper.

"I want to surrender," Erskine said quietly.

"What? What's that?"

"I want to surrender," Erskine repeated.

"What's the matter, Mister?" the policeman asked, leaning forward.

"I just killed a woman— Her body's in my apartment."

"All right, now. Just take it easy," the policeman said, coming from behind the tall desk. "You're sure that you're not drunk?"

"I'm not drunk."

"Do you realize what you just said to me?"

"Yes. I do."

The policeman frowned and stared at Erskine.

"You've never been in an institution, have you?"

"No."

"Where do you live?"

Erskine gave his address.

"What apartment?"

"10B."

The policeman pushed a buzzer and then looked at Erskine from his head to his feet.

"What kind of work do you do?"

"I'm a retired insurance man."

"Are you armed?"

"No," Erskine said, shaking his head.

Two other policemen came rushing forward.

"Give us the keys to your apartment," the first policeman said to Erskine.

Erskine surrendered his keys.

"This man says he killed a woman at this address," the policeman said, giving the other two policemen the keys and a slip of paper. "Get over there and see what it's all about . . ."

"Listen, the body's on the kitchen table," Erskine roused himself and spoke helpfully. He glanced at his watch. "I wish you'd try to get there quickly. The maid comes in in a few minutes and she oughtn't to see all that mess . . ."

The policemen looked at one another; then the two who had been summoned ran out.

"When did this happen?"

"About an hour ago."

"How did you kill her?"

"With a knife, a kitchen knife; a butcher knife, they call it."

The policeman stared a moment, then pointed to a chair. Erskine sat heavily and sighed. The policeman went to him and quickly patted his pockets.

"I'm not armed," Erskine said in surprise.

"You want a cigarette?"

"I don't smoke."

"Now, why did you kill this woman?"

"I don't know!"

"You had an argument?"

"Sort of ..."

"She was your woman?"

"Well ..."

"You were keeping her? Sleeping with her?"

"No."

"She was cheating on you?"

"No."

"You were living with her?"

"No."

"She was trying to trick you out of your money?"

"No."

"You're married?"

"No."

"Was there another woman involved in this? Was somebody jealous?"

"No." He coughed nervously. "It was just between me and the one I killed."

"Well, what happened?" the policeman demanded. "Don't you remember what you did?" The policeman smiled ironically. "You're not playing a game are you?"

The word "game" made Erskine start slightly. Involuntarily his left hand reached inside his coat and he touched the tip ends of the four, automatic colored pencils clipped there ... Slowly his eyes widened. He no longer heard the policeman's voice; he was staring at yet another memory from the dusty past, a nebulous memory whose return stunned him even more than had his recollection of that battered doll, for this memory now told him that his previous memory of that battered doll was but the *memory of a dream he'd had!*

He'd never "killed" the doll, really! That memory was but the recalling of a shameful daydream of revenge which he had pushed out of his mind! It was what he had angrily daydreamed one day when he'd been playing games with Gladys and her dolls; they'd been coloring paper with colored pencils and he'd drawn the image of a dead, broken doll and he had imagined Gladys telling on him and his mother branding him as bad ... He'd pictured vividly to himself what he'd wanted to do to his mother for having gone off and left that night when he'd been ill ... He now understood the four pencils!

His lips parted in horror as his memory spanned the void of time and revealed the reality of what he had done. He stared about as though drugged, unaware of the policeman and the barred windows ...

"Don't you hear me talking to you?" the policeman asked.

"Hunh?" Erskine grunted, struggling to orient himself.

"Tell me what happened!" the policeman shouted at him.

How could he ever explain that a daydream buried under the rigorous fiats of duty had been called forth from its thirty-six-year-old grave by a woman called Mabel Blake, and that that taunting dream had so overwhelmed him with a sense of guilt compounded of a reality which was strange and alien and which he loathed, but which, at the same time, was astonishingly familiar to him: a guilty dream which he had wanted to disown and forget, but which he had had to reenact in order to make its memory and reality clear to him! He closed his eyes in despair ... still touching the four colored pencils!

"You won't talk, hunh?" the policeman was asking.

"I've confessed," Erskine mumbled. "Your men will find her body soon. That's all I'm going to say; it's all I'm *ever* going to say ..." His voice trailed off uncertainly.

"That's your right, of course," the policeman said. "But it's always better to come clean. You've told the most important thing. It's better for you to tell it all, Mr.... What's your name?"

"Fowler; Erskine Fowler."

Erskine readily identified himself, his business connections, his church and club memberships; he even tendered his bank book. The policeman gaped.

"Mr. Fowler, you look like a solid citizen to me. Tell me, what's behind all this?"

"I've told you all that I'm going to tell," Erskine said.

"Was the woman pregnant?"

"Not that I know of ... Not by me, at least."

"How long did you know this woman?"

"Really, only two days."

"*Two days?* What happened? Tell me what happened ... I can help you, maybe ..."

"I can tell you nothing."

"You're scared to tell?"

"No."

"Then you *won't* tell?"

"I *can't* tell."

"Why?"

"Oh, I don't know ... Leave me alone!"

There was silence. The policeman stared at Erskine.

"Empty your pockets on that table there ..."

Erskine obeyed.

"That's everything?"

"That's everything."

"And you won't talk?"

Erskine shook his head and mumbled: "I *can't* talk."

The phone rang. The policeman picked it up, his eyes still fixed intently upon Erskine's face. The policeman frowned as he listened.

"Notify the Medical Examiner at once," he issued instructions into the phone. "I'm sending over the Homicide Squad right away ... Stick close there and don't let anybody touch anything." He listened further and then hung up.

"The officers at your apartment have learned that this woman's son was killed accidentally two days ago," the policeman said. "Do you know anything about that?"

"I can't tell you anything," Erskine said; he bowed his head in his arms.

END

AFTERWORD

African-American literary critic Bernard Bell dismissed Richard Wright's 1954 novel, *Savage Holiday*, as "a melodramatic Freudian tale of the repressed sexuality of [protagonist] Erskine Fowler."[1] But his description misses the importance of the point it makes: that Wright was interested in writing a novel so explicitly psychoanalytic that it would resemble a case study. This book was yet another expression (albeit an experimental one in his use of white characters) of his intense, lifelong, and unsentimental interest in exploring the human soul, the position of women in modern western culture, and the pathological aspects of various forms of repression.

"The protagonist is called Erskine Fowler," said Wright in a 1956 interview about *Savage Holiday*. "He is a rather wealthy New York insurance agent in his forties. He is white. But, as his name indicates, his problem is mostly moral, or it has been defined in terms of social morality. Fowler brings to one's mind the notion of being 'foul,' of defiling, of not behaving according to social rules."[2] The issue of social morality or social conventions is complicated here by a welter of psychosocial and psychosexual pathologies rooted in religion, family, and work, the constituents of both society and culture. *Savage Holiday* is about, among other things, matricide—the destruction of the being who holds those constituents together.

Richard Wright was born in 1908, the same decade in
which Americans first took flight in a power-driven air-
plane, and he died in 1960, a few years after the launching
of Sputnik and the beginning of the great space race. Put
another way, Wright was born in the social science age of
Durkheim and William James, and he died during the era
of David Reisman and Eliot Liebow. He entered a world of
pragmatism and social Darwinism and left one of existen-
tialism and the beginnings of postmodernism. These his-
torical references are not inappropriate in a discussion of
this great American author's life. I can think of no African-
American writer, before or since, who believed so unyield-
ingly that the culture of the industrialized west was scientific—that it was governed by scientific sensibilities and
preoccupations—and who so consistently saw the world in
rigorously unsentimental terms, whose thinking was both
metaphilosophical and psychosociological. It is significant
that he once said in a 1955 interview that his heroes were
"medical and scientific ones: Einstein, Pasteur, etc.," in addition to the literary figures one would expect a writer to
mention.[3] For Wright, unabashedly, modernity meant the
establishment of scientific, rational inquiry into the nature
of things. He was drawn to Marxism, sociology, and psychology because such forms of inquiry aided his search
within as a novelist. The struggle of modern man, as
Wright saw it, was to combat the atavistic, irrational impulses that reflected the irrationality of the society and culture in which he lived. Thus he undertook to explore in
Savage Holiday subjects that interested him: matricide, sexual repression in western religion, and sexual license in sec-
ularized western culture. In part, his interest in these ideas
developed because he was not a product of the higher education of his caste. College education for African Americans in the 1920s was for the most part still steeped in
Christian piety and Victorian morality. On the other hand,

Wright was very much a product of his age, insofar as science was believed to be man's (and the west's) most glorious achievement.

It seems clear that Wright had become far more ardent about sociology and psychology than about Marxism by the 1950s. Simply put, the questions that continued to be of interest to him in this small novel, as in much of his other work, are: What is freedom and what is desire? Why do human beings find it so confounding, even destructive, to seek and use their freedom, to understand the nature of their desire? What is it that human beings will for themselves and why is human will so flawed? Speaking in an interview about *Savage Holiday*, Wright gives this account of how the book came to be: "Maybe I can explain to you how I came across this idea. I had entered a library and was glancing at books naturally, casually, without any purpose. I came across a passage dealing with the problem of freedom. Not in a philosophical sense but a practical sense."[4] This problem of freedom, or as Wright restates it with the help of the interviewer, of leisure, is simply illustrated not only by Wright's discovery in whatever book he found but by the act itself, his own leisurely browsing in the library. The casual causality of the book, as Wright relates its coming into being, is itself a comment on the subject of the book and on the author's relationship to his tragic protagonist.

Savage Holiday appeared during Wright's self-imposed exile in Europe, where he lived from 1946 until his death in 1960. The books he wrote during those years have generally been either ignored by critics or damned with faint praise. It might be said that Richard Wright was a writer of such magnitude that he himself could elicit an extraordinary amount of public attention while his work suffered utter neglect. *Black Boy*, *Native Son*, and *Uncle Tom's Children*, written and published in America between 1937 and

1945, had, by the 1950s, become his best-known works, and they continue, to this day, to be the most canonized and frequently taught. Yet it was during the post-World War II exile that Wright produced most of his books, displaying an extraordinary diversity of interest; he became, in many ways, a "world" writer, or a writer with far-reaching concerns, as he began to feel more a citizen of the world than of a particular nation or the prisoner of a race. He was also, by 1953, as Michel Fabre writes, "a novelist with an international audience, an 'established writer' and what could be called a Parisian intellectual."[5] "I have no religion in the formal sense of the word," Wright tells a Spanish woman early on in *Pagan Spain*. "I have no race except that which is forced upon me. I have no country except that to which I'm obliged to belong. I have no traditions. I'm free. I have only the future."[6] Was he simply an uprooted, marginal man, or had he willed himself into a new being, reinventing himself as a western man of color?

During the postwar exile period, Wright's novels *The Outsider* and *The Long Dream* were published in addition to *Savage Holiday*. His major nonfiction works *Black Power*, *Pagan Spain*, and *The Color Curtain* also appeared, as well as a book of essays on the emerging Third World entitled *White Man, Listen!* and a collection of stories (some written before the 1950s), *Eight Men*. He had also written the script for and starred in the 1950 film version of *Native Son*, which was wretchedly edited for release in this country but was nonetheless a vital achievement for any author, especially an African American. That Wright was fascinated by cinema (although he thoroughly distrusted it, as he did much of popular culture) can be seen from passages involving movie-watching in *Native Son*, *Black Boy*, and *Black Power*. He must have been enormously impressed by the potential powers of cinema when he saw *Native Son* transformed partly through his own efforts as *auteur*.[7]

Thus, in many respects, the postwar years were not only the most productive ones for Wright but may also be the most crucial in our understanding of his ambition and aspiration as an artist.

The publication in 1954 of a novel by Wright that featured only white characters was not so unusual; such works by several noted black writers had already appeared. Zora Neale Hurston, Ann Petry, Chester Himes, William Attaway, Willard Motley, and Frank Yerby had all written "white" novels that predated Wright's book. Two years later, James Baldwin's remarkable and controversial novel, *Giovanni's Room*, with white homosexual characters, would be published. And, certainly, the famous "passing" novels of Charles Chesnutt and James Weldon Johnson contained a substantial number of white characters. So, if writing the white, or predominantly white, novel was not a tradition among black writers by the mid-1950s, it was clearly an established practice. "I tried to tell the story," Wright said in an interview about *Savage Holiday* in 1960, "of a white person. I picked a white American businessman to attempt a demonstration about a universal problem."[8] Like Baldwin and others, Wright wanted to write about something "universal" without its being obscured by the particularism of race. The creation of a black protagonist would have mired the book in a discussion about race among its reviewers and critics, especially in America. Certainly, the critical failure, in both black and white circles, in America of *The Outsider*, published a year before *Savage Holiday* and featuring a black antihero who explicitly denounced any sense of racial consciousness, could be attributed in part to the debate over the relevance or role of race in the book.

The plot of *Savage Holiday* is straightforward enough. At the age of forty-three, Erskine Fowler is forced to retire from the Longevity Life Insurance Company, which he helped to build, after twenty years of service, because he is,

as he is told by one of the other executives, "out of date,
behind the times." "[You're] good, Fowler. But, god-
dammit, you're not good enough!" He is being replaced by
"young Warren who was from Harvard and had studied insurance scientifically." Having lived solely for work all his
life, he must now adjust to his holiday, an idea that discom-
forts him greatly. At his apartment on a Sunday morning,
undressed for his shower, he tries to grab his morning
paper while naked but is shut out of his apartment. In a
panic, Fowler tries desperately to find the superintendent
of the building, riding madly up and down the elevator
while frantically trying to avoid meeting anyone, repelled
by the sight of his own body: "His hairy body, as he
glanced down at it, seemed huge and repulsive, like that of
a giant; but, when he looked off, his body felt puny, shriveled, like that of a dwarf." Calling up associations of Gul-
liver and Alice, Wright presents the dilemma of modern
man, dramatized in miniature by Fowler's mad flight,
naked, around the apartment building, in which the protagonist tries to escape the public revelation of what he is.
As a powerful giant, he is ugly, ape-like; inverted, he is
helplessly small. In either instance, he is misshapen and out
of place in his own world, the apartment building—an aes-
thetic, economic, and social structure that implies, even en-
courages, community while thwarting the very possibility
of its ever being achieved. Stripped of his few garments
of civilization and social status, Fowler wants to hide,
ashamed of what he feels he truly is and fearful of being revealed to others. He finally remembers he can reach his
bathroom window by climbing from an adjacent balcony.
Unfortunately, Tony Blake, the son of a tenant and widow
named Mabel, is playing on the balcony. The boy, whom
Fowler had befriended and knew well, is so shocked to see
the sweating, bewildered naked form, "his long, hairy arms
flaying the air rapaciously, like the paws of a huge beast

clutching for something to devour, to rend to pieces," that he falls from the balcony to his death ten stories below.

Through a combination of guilt, fear, and sexual attraction, Fowler becomes involved with Mabel, one of Wright's most intriguing female creations. Though he hates her, thinking she is nothing more than a tramp and a whore, he is also sexually attracted to her and tells himself that through marriage, he can bring her back to bourgeois, Christian respectability. Fowler, the reader learns, has had little contact with women during his life; he is both haunted by the memory of a mother who was much like Mabel and trapped by the compulsive conventionality of his stodgy sanctimonious Christianity. Her fate is sealed when, near the novel's end, in answer to Erskine's question as to how she could not love her son, she says that "it's not in my nature to be a mother" and "Erskine, I'm no mother." "What a cold monster of a woman!" Erskine thinks right before he murders her. The novel ends with his turning himself in to the police.

Wright, with his bent toward scientific consideration of his subject, was obviously influenced by psychiatrist Frederic Wertham's *Dark Legend: A Study in Murder*, an account of Gino, an Italian immigrant boy who murders his mother.[9] But he was probably even more deeply influenced by the general cultural view in the 1950s in both psychiatric and popular circles that whatever was wrong with the American male—with males generally—was the fault of the mother. It was the era of Momism. A number of films in the 1950s dealt with overbearing motherhood and femininity, from *My Son, John* to *Psycho*.[10] Momism is, as Erik Erikson explains, related to puritanism, an important association in Wright's novel. Erikson writes:

> During the short course of American history rapid developments fused with puritanism in such a way that they contributed to the emotional tension of mother

and child. Among these were the continued migration of the native population, unchecked immigration, industrialization, urbanization, class stratification, and female emancipation. These are some of the influences which put puritanism on the defensive—and a system is apt to become rigid when it becomes defensive. Puritanism, beyond defining sexual sin for full-blooded and strong-willed people, gradually extended itself to the total sphere of bodily living, compromising all sensuality—including marital relationships—and spreading its frigidity over the tasks of pregnancy, childbirth, nursing, and training. The result was that men were born who failed to learn from their mothers to love the goodness of sensuality before they learned to hate its sinful uses. Instead of hating sin, they learned to mistrust life. Many became puritans without faith or zest.[11]

The novel explores this issue beyond the matter of Fowler's pharisaical conceit. In the boy Tony Blake, we see culture at work in the creation of the male psyche. Frightened by his misperceptions of his mother's sexual relations, which he thinks is a form of combat, Tony does not wish to grow up because "I don't wanna fight ladies like my mother." (It is not irrelevant to Tony's "sexual pacifism" that his biological father, Mabel's husband, died in the war, a man-made creation that allows the father always to be a son and that leaves women and children bereft and abandoned. Ironically, Tony expresses the wish to his mother that Fowler could be his father. Wright complicates this issue by making Tony ambivalent about the notion of "father"; he is both frightened and solace-seeking, unlike Gino in *Dark Legend*: "The father-image became for Gino the symbol of happiness and the emblem of his tribulations: 'I haven't had a moment of pleasure since my father died.' "[12]) Thus, in young Tony's mind, war is equated with sex and family, with the relationship between men and women. Wright makes this explicit when he has Tony ask

Fowler, who offers to buy him a toy, for two fighter bombers, "[the] kind that carries the atom bomb." " 'Two?' Erskine had asked. 'But why two?' 'I wanna mama bomber and a papa bomber, and the little baby bombers with 'em,' Tony had explained."

In the novel, the notions of unbridled female sensuality that can only be contained through the strictures of motherhood and home and a constrained male desire, directed to work and war, become mutually supportive views of a contradictory reality, illustrative and worshipful both of that which regenerates the race and that which destroys it. On an Oedipal level, Fowler, Tony, and Mabel make up a nuclear family that is destroyed by Fowler, the father, who kills the son because he is the product of sexuality and murders the mother because she evokes it. As Erikson writes: "For, if you come down to it, Momism is only misplaced paternalism."[13] Men abdicate their roles as fathers so that they might always be sons, which is precisely what Fowler has remained all his life: a haunted, anxiety-ridden son murdering the mother who failed to be both mother and father to him so that he could reinvent her as a being beyond the sensuality that so threatens him.

There is much religious symbolism and imagery in this novel, which is not unusual in Wright's work. Despite being an atheist, he was drawn to Christianity for much the same reason Schopenhauer was: because it provides a rich set of expressions and metaphors about the essential pessimism of human existence. Examples in the novel include Fowler's calling his fellow employees at Longevity Life "brothers and sisters" in his farewell speech; his referring to the act of insuring people not as a business but as a faith; Tony's fall from the balcony, a fall from grace and innocence that ultimately takes both Mabel and Fowler with him; and the ritual, sacrificial stabbing of Mabel, who, as a perverted Christ symbol, must die for her own sins as well

as Fowler's. But Wright is just as preoccupied with what
philosopher Sidney Hook describes as the obsessions of
Dostoyevsky, a writer who not only influenced Wright
deeply but to whom he was sometimes compared. Dostoyevsky's concerns, according to Hook, were "the existence of evil; the validity of objective ethical standards as
against ethical solipsism, and the question of moral responsibility."[14] These were major themes in all of Wright's
fiction but especially in the works of the early 1950s. In *The
Outsider*, for instance, a novel that Michel Fabre rightly
connects to *Savage Holiday*, Wright's particular investigation of the character of Cross Damon leads, finally and ve-
hemently, to a rejection of Cross's ethical solipsism and
evasion of moral responsibility, each largely coming as a
result of the other. Cross, in his innocence, is as evil as the
evil he tries to destroy, not because he wishes to destroy it
but because his action results from selfish, vain whim, not
from solidarity with others or a desire for such solidarity.
In *Savage Holiday*, Wright returns to the same themes with
something of a different test case: Fowler is guilty of ethical solipsism stemming from his puritanism and self-made
Americanism. He tries to avoid responsibility for the death
of Tony by blaming Tony's "bad" mother. Actually,
Fowler's evil is ultimately less heroic than Cross Damon's
because his struggle is much less epic. While Damon seems
larger than life, Fowler is merely prosaic. The insurance
man/priest (and what else is a minister in a sense but a spir-
itual insurance agent?), Fowler, knows that you cannot
learn about evil from books. His belief that "you just had to
know in your heart that man was a guilty creature" is a
Calvinist view of the world if there ever was one. *Savage
Holiday* has much in common with Hawthorne's *The Scarlet
Letter*, also a novel about the censuring of women, the sup-
pression of family, and betrayal by the father.
    Wright originally saw *Savage Holiday* as the first novel in

an ambitious trilogy. The second, to be called "Strange Daughter," was to have as its subject a white American girl working through her sexual repression in a perverted relationship with a Nigerian and her subsequent murder. The third, "When the World Was Red," was to be an exploration of the psyche of the Aztec ruler Montezuma, as well as a psychohistory of western religion at the time of the Cortez expedition. This was not the first time that Wright had envisioned writing a series of thematically related novels, and, as before, the project was never completed. One of Wright's problems during the 1950s was that he suffered from severe bouts of writer's block where fiction was concerned—one reason, though not the only one, that he turned increasingly to nonfiction writing. Even so, he was still able during this decade to complete a considerable amount of fiction, including *The Long Dream*, *Rite of Passage* (started as "The Jackal" in 1944), and the still-unpublished "Island of Hallucinations." Another difficulty for Wright, because of the increasingly negative critical attention his work was receiving in the United States during this time, was finding publishers who were interested in his work. Even though the trilogy was never completed, however, it is important for us as readers to know the context in which Wright imagined *Savage Holiday* and the larger creative implications and possibilities he saw in its themes. Far from being a little Freudian potboiler, the novel was for Wright the first step in a thoroughgoing critique of the religious foundations of the western mind.

The return of *Savage Holiday* to print gives readers the opportunity to consider some important aspects of the work of this major American writer: his continuing development of the theme of religious obsession with guilt and sexual repression in a liberating set of circumstances; his use of white characters as a means of challenging himself in his craft; his exploration of the idea of a man's work being taken away because he was "out of style" and deemed no longer relevant, a particularly important point in understanding Wright's professional and personal struggles in the 1950s. This small, dense novel is another significant key to an understanding of the magnitude of Wright's literary achievement and to an acknowledgement of the complex passion of his sense of engagement. Perhaps it will at last find its rightful place in the Wright canon, in the canon of American literature.

Gerald Early
Washington University

NOTES

1. Bernard W. Bell, *The Afro-American Novel and Its Tradition* (Amherst: The University of Massachusetts Press, 1987), p. 189.

2. Keneth Kinnamon and Michel Fabre, eds., *Conversations with Richard Wright* (Jackson: University Press of Mississippi, 1993), p. 167.

3. Kinnamon and Fabre, *Conversations*, p. 165.

4. Kinnamon and Fabre, *Conversations*, p. 236.

5. Michel Fabre, *The Unfinished Quest of Richard Wright* (Urbana: University of Illinois Press, 1993), p. 382.

6. Richard Wright, *Pagan Spain* (London: The Bodley Head, 1960), p. 23.

7. The full story of the making of the film *Native Son* is found in Fabre, *Unfinished Quest*, pp. 336-53.

8. Kinnamon and Fabre, *Conversations*, p. 167.

9. Frederic Wertham, *Dark Legend: A Study in Murder* (London: Victor Gollancz Ltd., 1947). Other sources for *Savage Holiday* are mentioned in Fabre, *Unfinished Quest*, pp. 376-80.

10. Michael Rogin, "Kiss Me Deadly: Communism, Motherhood, and Cold War Movies," in *Ronald Reagan: The Movie* (Berkeley: University of California Press, 1987), pp. 236-71.

11. Erik Erikson, *Childhood and Society*, 2d ed. (New York: Norton, 1963), pp. 292-93. For the full account of Momism, see pp. 288-96.

12. Wertham, *Dark Legend*, p. 83.

13. Erikson, *Childhood and Society*, p. 295.

14. Sidney Hook, "The Ethics of Suicide," in *Convictions* (Buffalo, New York: Prometheus Books, 1990), p. 43.